THE COWBOY'S
Christmas Reunion

VALERIE COMER

Greenwords Media

Cover Art © 2018 Lynnette Bonner, www.indiecoverdesign.com.

Period Images 2015-11-18_15.49.31 (cowboy)

Shutterstock 130722278 (red barn in snow)

The lyrics to *Joy to the World* are found in the public domain.

First edition, GreenWords Media, 2018

Valerie Comer Bibliography

Urban Farm Fresh Romance

0. Promise of Peppermint (ebook only)
1. Secrets of Sunbeams
2. Butterflies on Breezes
3. Memories of Mist
4. Wishes on Wildflowers
5. Flavors of Forever
6. Raindrops on Radishes
7. Dancing at Daybreak

Saddle Springs Romance

1. The Cowboy's Christmas Reunion
2. The Cowboy's Mixed-Up Matchmaker
3. The Cowboy's Romantic Dreamer
4. The Cowboy's Convenient Marriage

Christmas in Montana Romance

1. More Than a Tiara
2. Other Than a Halo
3. Better Than a Crown

Garden Grown Romance
(Arcadia Valley Romance)

1. Sown in Love (ebook only)
2. Sprouts of Love
3. Rooted in Love
4. Harvest of Love

Farm Fresh Romance

1. Raspberries and Vinegar
2. Wild Mint Tea
3. Sweetened with Honey
4. Dandelions for Dinner
5. Plum Upside Down
6. Berry on Top

Riverbend Romance Novellas

1. Secretly Yours
2. Pinky Promise
3. Sweet Serenade
4. Team Bride
5. Merry Kisses

valeriecomer.com/books

So how many households does that make?" Kade Delgado shifted his sleeping toddler in his arms, but Jericho snored on.

His buddy James Carmichael tapped a pen to his notebook. "Fifteen, including seven single moms with eighteen kids under the age of ten." He looked around the trio of cowboys. "Can we handle that many?"

"We can if Kade's brothers are in." Garret Morrison raised his eyebrows at Kade.

"Not sure if Sawyer is sticking around." The onset of winter might send his kid brother south, and the weatherman had called for an early storm. A glance out the window proved the forecast correct. A swirl of blowing snow peppered the glass, faintly illuminated by the lighted coffee shop sign.

Man, Kade should have come to Saddle Springs for groceries yesterday, but an injured heifer had kept him tied up. Or he should have denied his buddies' invitation to coffee while he was in town anyway. This could have been handled by email, couldn't it? He really needed to get going. The mountain road would be beyond sketchy and all the way to ugly soon — if it wasn't already.

"I'll have to double-check with both of them, but what's the alternative? Let some kid wake up with no gifts on Christmas morning?" Kade's arms tightened around his young son. "Let some old man or young mom struggle to shovel themselves out after a snowstorm — which, by the way, we're getting the mother of right now? Let's wrap this up."

Garret nodded. "Break them up geographically. I'll take the ones on the east side of town. That includes—" he leaned closer to James's notebook and circled part of the page with his finger "—Granny Talcott and the Yang family. Carmen Haviland. A couple more."

Geographically? Kade shook his head but didn't voice his thoughts. It only made sense, but that gave him the Mackenzies. They'd been reclusive even before their granddaughter, Cheri, had skipped town less than a week prior to her wedding to Kade and never looked back. Her choice sent her grandparents into a spin they hadn't recovered from in over six years. Neither had Kade. Not really.

He forced his mind back to the cozy coffee shop and nuzzled the top of Jericho's tousled head. It was past time to get all the way over Cheri. To man up and give her grandparents a good dose of Jesus' love. Mend some fences, literally and otherwise.

James angled a look at him. "That okay, Kade?"

"Sure." Maybe he could sic one of his brothers on Cheri's grandparents. "Look, I'll be back in town in a few days, but I really need to get Jer home and check the cattle before this storm blows in for real." He poked his chin toward James as he rose. "Send me an email."

The two-year-old struggled in his arms and rubbed sleep out of his eyes. "Daddy?"

"Yes, bucko?"

"I hungry."

The middle-aged barista bustled over carrying a plate of treats. "Here, little man. Let Auntie Abigail give you a cookie. Daddy won't mind."

Kade chuckled. "You're sneaky, Abigail." He slid Jericho to the floor and reached for his cowboy hat. Abigail's rules included hats off inside Java Springs. "Only one, bucko. We'll have supper when we get back to the ranch."

"Tanku," Jericho announced, helping himself to a cookie and giving Abigail a shy smile.

She held the plate toward Kade. "Have a couple for the road. I think I'll lock up behind you guys, even though it's a little early. I imagine everyone in Saddle Springs will haul in an extra armload of firewood and hunker down for the storm."

"I don't mind if I do." Kade plucked a pumpkin cookie studded with cranberries off the plate. "Thanks. These are great."

She turned toward the other guys as they shrugged into their jackets. Kade pulled out his key fob, started his truck with a press of the button, then knelt to tug Jericho's parka around the boy before zipping it.

Behind him, the coffee shop door swung open with a jingle of bells and a blast of Arctic air. He glanced over his shoulder and froze as solid as the Montana night.

Framed in the doorway stood Cheri Mackenzie. The woman couldn't be anyone else. Her long blond hair, anchored with a dark knit hat, whipped in the snow-swirled wind, and a black wool coat covered her frame. Those blue eyes lassoed his like he was a faltering calf. The force of the shock was so great it took a second to realize a little girl who looked like her clung to her hand.

Didn't that just figure?

Kade rocked back on his heels and stood, pulling the brim of his cowboy hat down a smidgen. "Cheri. What a surprise."

James strode over and pulled the carved wooden door shut, but the newcomer didn't even seem to notice.

Maybe everyone else thought it was warmer in here without winter howling in, but it made no difference to Kade. The sight of her after all these years reminded him his heart had moved to the North Pole... and not to the cozy den housing Santa's workshop.

He hoisted Jericho into his arms and tore his gaze from hers long enough to nod to his friends. "See you."

"Can I pour you a coffee? Maybe get you some cookies?" Abigail bustled closer. "I was going to close up, but I can stay another half hour. Get you warmed up before you head back into this."

Cheri's eyes went from Kade's to Abigail's and back again. "My car is stuck."

Garret reached for his gloves. "Where about, ma'am? We can shovel you out. Get you on your way."

"It kind of slid off the highway when I turned into town." She bit her lip. "I'll need a tow truck, I think."

"Sully's gone down to Missoula early for Thanksgiving." Abigail glanced between the men with a worried frown. "And Danny's got a broken leg. I don't know as there's someone else who can drive that rig."

"Can haul it out with the tractor if needed," said Garret.

James thumbed toward the darkened window. "That's a job best done in daylight."

Everyone turned to Kade. Why, what did he have to do with this? Nothing. Nothing at all. Cheri had washed her hands of him and, after wallowing in disbelief and anger for a few weeks — okay, make that months — he'd washed his right back. He wasn't getting involved in anything within ten miles of Cheri Mackenzie ever again. In fact, he wouldn't even need to help out her grandparents for the Cowboy Santa project now that she was here. She could take care of them.

Except... didn't the mandate include single moms? But she probably wasn't single. Her husband had likely stayed by the car and sent her in to make a phone call.

Kade didn't have to lift a finger to help her. He swung Jericho to his left hip. "Sorry to hear of your troubles." Other than that they served her right. Being stuck in a snowbank was nothing compared to what she'd done to him.

"What brings you back to Saddle Springs?" Abigail asked.

Kade stared at Cheri, eyebrows raised. Wasn't that the question they all wanted the answer to? Other than Garret, who hadn't lived here back then.

Her gaze darted to his then back to Abigail. "Grandpa needs me. He fell and broke some ribs a few days ago and can't really manage the chores."

Cheri was a hundred pounds at most, wearing boots and soaking wet. Didn't look like she'd put on any weight in the past six years. Unless she'd been doing some serious working out, she couldn't toss bales any more than Chester could. And weren't her grandparents down to two or three horses?

He sucked in his bottom lip. So much for the Mackenzies being off his list. Unless there really was a Mr. Cheri somewhere, but she kept saying *I* and *me*. Not *us* and *we*. Dead giveaway there.

"Your grandparents' spread is halfway up River Road, right?" put in James. "Kade is going right past on his way to Eaglecrest. He can probably drop you and your daughter off, and we can dig your car out tomorrow when the snow lets up."

"I couldn't ask."

Kade choked back a snort. She didn't have to, not with his buddies and Abigail being ever so helpful. His conscience bit hard. He'd forgiven her, hadn't he? If not, he'd at least moved on, in a manner of speaking.

Married Daniela. Been widowed, which was only another way to leave a guy standing there in his sock feet with his hat off, trying to sort out what had happened. And through it all, God had quietly smoothed out rough places in his life and filled the dry creek beds.

He gave a curt nod. "We can do that. Like James says, I'm going right past anyway." Because half an hour ago, he'd signed on to fulfill God's mandate to help the widows and fatherless in their distress. Wasn't it like God to make him start with Cheri Mackenzie?

THE WARM GLOW from the windows of the coffee shop where she'd hung out so often as a teen had burned a welcoming beacon to Cheri as she struggled up the street, towing her daughter through snow that seemed to deepen even in the three blocks from the highway turnoff. It had seemed cozy and welcoming right until she'd stepped inside and seen Kade Delgado. Holding a toddler.

Then the Montana winter wind swirled around her heart once again. What had she been thinking, coming home? That she could keep on sneaking through town to the ranch as she'd done occasionally over the years? That she could hide out there for a month or two, helping her grandparents, with neither the nosy town of Saddle Springs nor the Delgados at Eaglecrest Ranch up the road any the wiser?

Now Abigail Evening crouched in front of her daughter, offering her a cookie. Harmony whispered a thank you as she accepted.

Cheri took a deep breath. "I'll get a room at the Hats Off Motel. If it's still in business." Not that she wanted to. Not when Grandpa and Grandma were expecting her tonight, but it had to be better than spending twenty minutes in the cab of Kade's truck.

All eyes stared at her.

"But, Mama..." Harmony looked up at her, tears catching on the ends of her eyelashes.

"I can drive you." Kade's words were polite enough, but there was only steel in those brown eyes. "Chester can bring you down to get your car in a day or two. We'll leave a note for Sully and the State Patrol so they know it's not abandoned." He poked his chin toward the door. "Truck's already running just outside. Ready?"

She'd never be prepared, but she nodded anyway. "Thanks."

"That's settled, then." Abigail beamed like she'd directed the Helena Symphony. Maybe she thought she had.

Kade pushed the door open and held it, forcing Cheri to brush past him. Even with the snow battering her face, the scent she smelled was all Kade. Horses. Leather. And a hint of woodsy aftershave. Memories flooded her, memories she shoved aside. He had a kid. He was married. Off limits... not that she was exactly free herself.

The other two cowboys came out behind them, slapping backs and promising to keep in touch. And here she'd thought it was women who had hen parties.

Kade opened the passenger door of the big black Chevy idling at the curb then the door behind it. "Hop in," he said to Harmony, still holding his little guy. Always the gentleman. He shut the doors behind them both then rounded the truck and tucked his boy into the car seat. A minute later he was in the driver's seat. "Need anything from your car? Suitcase? Booster, maybe?"

"That would be helpful. Thank you."

A few minutes later, her bags in the truck bed, Kade flipped on the four-wheel drive and pointed the truck west across the bridge and up the mountain road. Swirling snow blocked visibility, but Cheri relaxed. At least she didn't have to drive in this mess anymore. She could trust Kade.

"So... your daughter." Kade flicked a glance into the rearview mirror.

Some wouldn't believe she wasn't Kade's child, but he knew. She knew. "Her name is Harmony. She'll be six in April." Let him do the math.

He shot her a tight glance barely discernible in the glow of the truck's instrument panel. "Who's her father?"

Yep, he'd done the math. Harmony had been born nine months after the wedding that hadn't happened. Cheri shook her head. She wasn't ready to go there with Kade. Dredge open the whole mess from that horrible summer. "Your son looks a lot like you."

His lips tightened. "His name is Jericho."

Jericho. Kade had always liked that name. Planned to

name his first son that since he'd been a teen. Memories of long kisses in the apple orchard amid glorious fragrant blossoms blocked out the blowing snow for just a moment. They'd shared their hopes and promises and dreams. Until she'd ruined everything.

She blinked the dark night back into focus. Flakes stabbed at the windshield as the four-by-four rounded one more curve in the climb out of Saddle Springs. "Congratulations," she whispered. "I hope you're very happy."

The truck slid a little and Kade's gloved hands tightened on the wheel. Was the grim set of his chin because of the road conditions, the shock of seeing her again... or because his life wasn't full of joy?

The gates of Paradise Creek Ranch ghosted from the darkness, and Kade turned his truck to crawl down the long drive. Cheri couldn't help the worry that he wouldn't make it back out again, but he was a good driver, and the truck seemed nearly new. She dared to breathe again when the lights of the old ranch house came into view.

"Here you go." Kade lifted the bags out of the back, set them on the porch, and brushed a couple of inches of snow off them.

"Thanks." She helped Harmony down as the door opened and Grandma peered out.

"Thank goodness you made it!"

Cheri wrapped her grandmother in a hug. "More like thank Kade. My car is stuck in town, but we can get it in a day or two."

Grandma's eyebrows shot up. "Kade Delgado?"

"Ma'am." He tipped his hat as he turned away. "I'll be on my way home now."

She flinched as though he'd struck her. "You can't."

Kade swung back toward Grandma. "Pardon me?"

"Chester is listening to the scanner. There's an avalanche across the road at mile eighteen, by the hairpin curve. Won't be anyone getting through tonight. Took down all the lines, too."

He opened his mouth, snapped it shut again, and stared at Cheri, his gaze burning into hers for a long moment. "It's too far back to town."

It had taken them nearly an hour to crawl the twenty-minute trip. There'd been a lot of silence that matched the weather, past chilly and on to deep freeze. And now Grandma was suggesting *what* exactly?

Kade's gaze swung to Grandma. "May I borrow Chester's snowmobile?"

"It's broke down. He ordered parts last week. You and your boy will need to stay the night, I guess."

Cheri winced at the graceless words, but Grandma was right. If the road up to Eaglecrest was blocked, he didn't have any choice. "Harmony can sleep with me tonight. That will leave the other bedroom for Kade and Jericho. Maybe it will all look better in daylight." She could only hope.

From the truck came the bellow of an unhappy toddler. Still Kade stood, looking from one to the other. Then he pulled a cell phone out of his pocket, glanced at it, rolled his eyes, and shoved it back in. There'd never been decent coverage deep in this valley.

"I'd be obliged, ma'am. Thank you."

Wait. What? Just like that she'd be spending another twelve hours or more in the same house as Kade Delgado?

No, please, Lord. Hadn't she been punished enough?

CHAPTER 2

K ade unbuckled Jericho then eyed the few groceries he'd picked up before meeting the guys. Thankfully that had included a box of diapers. He grabbed what he could wrangle along with his son and headed for the house. Hostile. Enemy territory.

Lord, I hope You know what You're doing.

The savory aroma of beef stew drifted over him as he stepped inside the older log home and let Jericho slide down beside Cheri's daughter, who sat on the floor removing her snow boots. The little girl looked up, assessing him.

Whatever had happened back then wasn't this child's fault. "Harmony, can you help Jericho with his jacket? I need to get some more stuff from the truck."

She bit her lip then nodded, patting the floor. "Sit, Jericho."

The little guy plopped down beside the girl and grinned up at her. Figured.

"I'll be right back." Kade made short work of bringing in the rest of his bags. No point in letting the food freeze, and maybe he could offer a few things to Edith for putting him and Jericho up for the night.

When he got back inside, the children had disappeared. Kade hung their coats and added his own shearling-lined denim jacket to a hook then yanked off his cowboy boots and set them on the stone floor. Lined Jericho's boots up beside his. He closed his eyes and took a deep breath. *Okay, God, here goes nothing.*

"Jer?" Kade entered the kitchen as all voices quieted and all eyes turned to him. He'd snag another moment's reprieve. "C'mere, bucko. Let's get a dry diaper on you."

With the task taken care of, Kade washed up in the bathroom's porcelain sink stained with rust marks. A dribble of water remained even when he tightened the tap, reinforcing his first impression that having Chester and Edith on his Cowboy Santa list was warranted. It had been a while since anyone had taken care of things around here. Looked like Paradise Creek Ranch could soak up any spare hours he could give them, but would the Mackenzies accept it from him?

Would it be better if he told them it was a ministry of Springs of Living Water Church, or if he did it as a neighbor? They'd never been churchgoers. They'd never warmed up to their neighbors at Eaglecrest Ranch, either, even when he and Cheri were dating. He'd have to play it by ear.

Or would it just look like he was trying to spend time with Cheri again? Kade wasn't sure his heart was up for it. Maybe he should get one of the other guys to take on this part of the project, after all.

God?

No answer.

When Kade reentered the kitchen, his son broke away and scrambled up on a chair beside Harmony. Kade turned toward Chester, sitting in one of the rockers flanking the wood stove. "Good evening, Mr. Mackenzie. Heard you took a tumble. Doing okay?"

The older man frowned at him. "I'm fine. Been hurt worse a thousand times."

Kade nodded, keeping the grin corralled. "Got any chores I can do for you tonight or in the morning?" He poked his chin toward the half empty wood box. "Maybe haul in some firewood?"

Chester shrugged. "If you want to, I cain't stop you."

Graciousness personified. "Sure. Still got a few horses around, don't you? They need oats tonight? Water?" Kade held his hands over the wood stove.

"Water's automatic so long as it don't freeze too hard." The old man winced as he shifted in the rocker. "They'd probably 'preciate a bit o' grain."

"I'll go out right after supper then. If you think of anything else that needs done, don't hesitate to say so."

The old man grunted.

"Stew's on," said Edith. "Want yours over there, Chester, or can you get up to the table?"

"I'm comin'."

Kade turned to see Cheri setting a few large books on one of the wooden chairs. Was she creating a booster for Jericho? That was kind of her.

"Here you go, little guy. Hope your mama isn't too worried about why you're not home tonight."

From over by the counter, Edith's head snapped up, and her gaze collided with Kade's.

Ignoring the grunts as Chester struggled to his feet, Kade crossed over to the table and lifted his son onto the makeshift booster. "Jericho's mother died in childbirth." Close enough to the truth. More than anything, he wanted to demand what happened to Harmony's father. Who was he? By the child's age, the deadbeat nearly had to be someone Kade knew.

"I'm sorry to hear that," came Cheri's quiet words.

Sincere? Not sincere? Man, he needed to stop trying to read things into her voice. Stop letting the sight and fragrance of her quicken his pulse. Too much divided them now, like two small children who only needed stability. Kids needed two parents, too, but Kade's mom filled in as much as she could with Jericho. Kade took a deep breath. He'd forgotten Cheri once before — or at least done his best — and he'd avoid getting entangled again.

Even with the Cowboy Santa program?

It was going to be tough to have a merry little Christmas himself this year, but he'd promised to give one to widows and orphans. For a reason that made as much sense as prodding an angry bull, that seemed to include Cheri and her daughter.

Her grandmother glowered as Cheri tugged on her jacket, but didn't take back her agreement to play *Go Fish* with Harmony for a few minutes before bed. Cheri needed to talk to Kade, and that was better done without her daughter or grandparents. He'd tucked his son into a backpack half an hour ago, swung it to his shoulders, and headed out the door.

Gone to do the chores. Wasn't that why *she* had come home? Her conscience bit. Grandpa's injury had only been a part of it. A miniscule part, if she were honest with herself. No, it had been Dillon, showing up at the Grace Greenhouse Children's Center where she worked, searching for her. Maybe God was looking after her, after all — it had been her day off, and her boss, Alaina, had told her the next morning. Was that really only two days ago?

Cheri had quit her job on the spot, gone home, and packed up everything she could load into her old Fiesta while Harmony sobbed beside her. Her car's nearly bald tires were no match for the ugly road conditions she'd soon encountered, but at least they'd been away from Dillon's search. He'd found her once. She'd be crazy to think he wouldn't follow her to Saddle Springs, but where else could she go? She had to stop running.

She slid open the massive stable door and inhaled the once-familiar aromas of horses, hay, and leather. In the dim light of a lone lightbulb, Kade stroked the neck of a chestnut who stretched over the rail and leaned hard into his hand.

Blaze. Cheri's mare. The traitor.

Kade's head snapped up, and his hand dropped to his side. Blaze bumped his shoulder, but he ignored the horse as his gaze lassoed Cheri's.

She pulled the stable door shut behind her. "Hey. I was just coming out to say hello to Blaze."

Kade backed away. "Have at it. I'm headed back to the house to put Jer to bed. Don't worry. I'll stay out of your way."

The little boy's forehead was buried in his daddy's sheepskin collar, his eyes closed and his knit cap askew.

Cheri's fingers itched to straighten it, so she shoved them deep in her coat pockets. "Can we talk? I need to tell you how sorry I am for how I left you."

Silence. Kade's eyebrows rose into the shadow of his cowboy hat.

"I-I made some mistakes. Big ones." He'd already figured out how big. The result was probably demanding fives from her great-grandmother right at the moment. "I didn't know what to do. I couldn't face you." She took a deep breath. "So I took the coward's way out. I ran."

"Leaving me to face the music alone and cancel everything at the last minute. With no idea what was going on."

She winced and poked the toe of her boot at a hay bale. "I'm sorry. But it looks like you didn't suffer too long."

His gaze pierced hers. "You don't know anything. Don't pretend you do."

Cheri took a step back. "You have a lovely son. You and your wife must have been very happy." Except he'd said she died giving birth. *Way to put your foot in your mouth, girl.*

Only the horses' soft nickers as they shifted around their stalls punctuated the long silence. Finally Kade shook his head and stepped away from Blaze with a little shrug.

"Is she... was she someone I knew?" Why it mattered, Cheri had no idea, but somehow it did. Had he been half in love with someone else even while engaged to her? He couldn't have been. He'd been all hers until she'd given herself to Dillon in a fit of who-knew-what.

"No." Kade's voice hardened as he crossed his arms over his chest. "Her name was Daniela, and she came to Saddle Springs about two years later."

"You must miss her a lot."

He huffed. "Stop, Cheri. Just stop."

What was that supposed to mean? Couldn't she have regrets? That was too bad. She had regrets aplenty. *If only* was the mantra of her life. She'd struggled to love Harmony, to accept the price of her biggest mistake. Somehow the helpless infant had won her over despite her anger and fear. Now she wouldn't trade her daughter for anything, but that had been a long time coming.

"Who's her father?"

Cheri heard the unspoken words: *who'd you throw me over for?* The off chance of running into Kade was why she'd avoided Saddle Springs as much as possible. Yeah, she'd come for a few days in the summer here and there but, until their health declined this past year, her grandparents had done most of the traveling. They were all she had left, and the ranch was the only place to go when she was running from Dillon.

She'd driven into Saddle Springs, slid off the highway, and run smack into Kade. The avoidance was over. Maybe it was for the best. Closure, and all that.

He took a few steps closer until he loomed over her, bitter espresso pooling in his deep brown eyes. "Who?"

Cheri poked her chin up and met his gaze. He couldn't make her say. He was too much of a gentleman to push her that far.

Kade's jaw firmed. "Let me take a guess. Dillon Scarborough. He left town as suddenly as you did and has been about as scarce ever since."

She wouldn't give anything away. She'd keep staring into Kade's eyes like he wasn't dissecting her fickle heart. But, oh, those deep eyes had always had the power to suck her in.

"I knew it." He swung away and slammed the heel of his hand into a timber post.

That had to hurt, but Kade didn't even wince or shake out his hand. He pierced her with a dark look and strode to the stable door before pivoting. The toddler in the carrier swung a little but didn't waken. "I have one more question, and that's *why*? What could Dillon offer you that I couldn't? We were getting married in a *week*, Cheri. I thought you loved me as much as I loved you. I honored you. Adored you. If you had cold feet, you could've told me. We'd have worked through things together. What did I do to deserve being jilted?"

Tears swarmed Cheri's eyes, but she blinked them back. "You didn't do anything, Kade. You didn't deserve how I treated you. I'm so, so sorry." It seemed she'd been saying that a lot, and yet it could never be enough to make up for the chasm between them. "It was a mistake. The biggest mistake I ever made was throwing away what I had with you."

Kade stalked a few steps closer, thumbs hooked through the belt loops of his trim-fitting jeans. "Don't even think there could ever be anything between us again. I've been left twice now. I can tell you flat out that Jericho and I are fine on our own. We're not looking for anyone, especially not someone we can't trust one hundred percent."

The nerve of him. She widened her stance to match his. "You're full of yourself, Kade Delgado. I wouldn't throw myself at you if you were the last man on earth."

His head jerked in a tight nod. "Guess we're on the same page, then, because that goes both ways and double for me. With any luck, I'll be out of here at daybreak, and you can go back to forgetting I ever existed." He yanked down the brim of his cowboy hat and slid the stable door open.

The wind howled in, accompanying a spray of icy pellets. The door slammed hard against the stop, cutting off the sound, the snow, the darkness. Cutting off any faint hope she might have had.

Shaking, she crossed the stable, slipped into Blaze's stall, and wrapped her arms around the mare's neck. Salty tears poured into the blond mane as Blaze nuzzled her. Wasn't this the spot where Kade had rubbed?

Cheri cried harder, gulping for air. What had she expected? That there'd be room in Kade's heart for forgiveness? For mercy?

Even Jesus seemed to find it hard to forgive her. Kade was only a man. How could he forgive when God Himself struggled? She should've known better. Her grandparents were getting old — she hadn't realized how much they'd aged in the six months since she'd seen them last. She'd talk them into selling the ranch and moving to a small house in a town far, far away. She'd find a job nearby and care for them as long as she could.

And when they passed on, she'd be alone with Harmony. For the rest of her life.

CHAPTER 3

J ericho pounced on him and poked his ribs with blunt baby fingers. "Daddy! I hungry."

Kade rolled over on the narrow bed and captured his son, tickling the little guy until he squealed with delight. Only then did he let his gaze slip to the digital clock on the bedside table. The face was blank.

The power was out.

Of course. With a storm like last night's, it was pretty much a given this far back into the mountains. Hopefully Chester's generator was in good working order with enough fuel to run the thing for a day or two. By the dripping of the bathroom taps, the broken down snowmobile, and the messy heap of unchopped logs outside, Kade couldn't be certain. He'd split enough to fill the wood box last night. Swinging the axe had helped work out some of the frustration the conversation in the stable had brought to the surface.

Jericho bounced on Kade's chest. "Daddy, I—"

"Hungry. I know, bucko." Kade reached for his phone and turned on the flashlight app. "Let's change your diaper and go round up some breakfast." Thank the Lord he'd had groceries in the truck. Being dependent on Chester and Edith would not sit well. Not for him and, no doubt, not for them.

A few minutes later he padded down the short hallway, carrying Jericho. Someone had been up, as a lit kerosene lamp sat in the center of the table. Kade glanced at the kitchen range. Propane. Good. At least he didn't have to cook on the wood stove, although he could if he had to. He shone his flashlight app into the fridge, pulled out the bacon and a carton of eggs, and got started. Jericho dragged a chair over and climbed up to watch.

Soon the sizzle and aroma of cooking bacon filled the air. A whisper of sound came from the hallway, and Kade glanced over to see Harmony plodding in, wearing fuzzy pajamas and rubbing sleep out of her eyes.

Jericho clambered off the chair, ran to her, and squeezed her around the middle. "Ha'mony! Is morning."

Kade wasn't sure he'd go quite that far. The sky was still unrelentingly black, even though his watch told him it was past seven. He hadn't quite dared go out on the porch yet to see how much snow had fallen or what the damage might be. Better to assess in daylight, and there'd be no inkling of that for another hour or so.

"Good morning, Harmony. I hope you slept well."

She blinked over at him. "Good morning, Mr. Kade. Why don't you turn the lights on?"

Kade chuckled. That question alone told him Cheri had left her rural roots far behind. "Power's out. Are you hungry? Want some breakfast?"

The little girl's nose wrinkled. "Maybe cereal."

"You'll have to find it, then." No way was he prowling through Edith's cupboards. "If you want bacon and eggs, I'll serve you up." Those had come out of his own stash. "I can even make you some toast, if you like."

She edged closer, Jericho still clinging to her. Little traitor. "Doesn't the toaster plug into the wall?"

"Sure does, but I can make it on the stove. Want to see?"

"Toast, Daddy?" Jericho climbed back on the chair while Harmony leaned beside him.

Kade lit a second burner, let it heat, then turned it to low before laying a slice of bread over the cast iron grate. When the piece had gently browned, he flipped it with a fork before scooting the bacon aside and cracking in several eggs. When the second side had browned, he set another slice on the grate and buttered the first.

"Jericho, climb up on your booster. I'll bring you breakfast. Then do you want some, Miss Harmony?"

The little girl watched him with wide eyes. "Yes, please. I didn't know you could make toast like that."

He'd served both kids and was plating his own when Chester ambled into the kitchen, taking in the scene. Kade held the plate out. "Would you like breakfast, Mr. Mackenzie?"

Chester glanced over his shoulder. "Edith generally makes porridge."

"You're welcome to wait for her, if you like, but I have a few packs of bacon and a few dozen eggs in your fridge, and I'm happy to share."

"Does smell mighty fine."

Kade grinned. "Here you go, then. I'll fix myself some more. It will just take a minute. The pan's still hot."

The old man winced as he pulled out the chair at the head of the table. "Obliged."

Kade was still at the stove when Edith and Cheri entered the room, talking quietly to each other. His hand stopped moving, the flipper poised over the eggs. His stomach growled, seeming to realize it would be put off once again. *Lord, keep me gracious. There's more need in this house than I ever suspected.* He turned, steeling himself against the sight of Cheri in comfy gray sweats, her long hair loosely braided.

Her gaze shot to his, and his gut clenched, this time not from hunger. She was just as gorgeous as she'd been seven years ago when he'd proposed. There'd been no doubt in his mind that she was the woman for him, always and forever.

He'd been duped back then, but that wouldn't happen again, no matter how the electricity zinged between them. Last night, words had zinged, too. She'd ditched him years back and, last night, she'd reiterated her feelings. She didn't want him. The rejection stabbed all over again.

Two small children sat at the table, proof that six and a half years had, indeed, gone by. Their lives had diverged, and this chance meeting was only a reminder that a guy could never go back. Even though, yes, he wanted to forget all the hardship in between. He wanted to gather Cheri in his arms, forgive her, and carry on.

You're full of yourself, Kade Delgado. I wouldn't throw myself at you if you were the last man on earth.

That was what she really thought of him. There was no moving forward together. Just apart. Yesterday morning he'd been fine with that. Being a single father wasn't the easiest thing he'd ever done, but Jericho meant the world to him. Kade took him nearly every-where — in front of him in the saddle, in the pack on his back, in the truck's car seat. Jericho was his little buddy, and they'd make it through without a woman in their lives. Hadn't Kade already done the hard part alone, grieving Daniela while caring for a needy newborn?

The smell of eggs caught his attention, and he turned back to the cast iron skillet. Yeah, a bit overdone, but they would be fine, though his appetite had fled.

"WANT BACON AND EGGS?"

Cheri nearly stumbled when Kade pulled his atten-tion away from her and turned back to the stove. What had been going through his mind? She might have hurled nasty words at him last night, but she hadn't meant them. Okay, she'd meant the sorry part, but not the rest.

Beside her, Grandma sniffed. "I'll put on a pot of coffee in the percolator."

"Sounds good, Mrs. Mackenzie." Kade kept his back

to her. "I wasn't sure where you kept the grounds, or I'd have done it myself."

Mr. Self Sufficient had made himself right at home. A guy like Kade didn't need permission — or a hookup from NorthWestern Energy — to whip up breakfast. Not him. He stepped in and did what needed to be done: feeding the horses, hauling in wood, fixing a meal.

Grandma stepped over to the sink and turned on the tap. Nothing came out.

Cheri stifled a groan. Of course not. The water pump ran on electricity, too.

Kade glanced over at Grandpa as he plated his breakfast. "Generator fueled and ready to go?"

Grandpa nodded. "In the lean-to out back."

"I'll go get it started, then. May I leave Jericho in here?" Kade's gaze found Cheri's.

He'd made her daughter breakfast and still felt he had to ask? "Sure. He'll be fine." The boy had the appetite of a little cowpoke by the looks of his bowl.

"Eat your food while it's hot." Grandma pointed at Kade's plate. "The generator can wait five minutes."

He grinned at Grandma. "You said something about coffee."

"Eat first. Want some oatmeal, Cheri?"

"Um." What she really wanted was yogurt and fruit, but she already knew Grandma's opinion on a breakfast that needed to stick to her ribs. At Paradise Creek Ranch, a woman didn't get away with yogurt. She sighed. "Sure. Sounds good."

Kade dropped into the chair beside his son and made

quick work of his bacon, eggs, and toast before rising again. He rumpled Jericho's brown hair. "Be right back, bucko. Be good for Miss Cheri."

The little boy offered Cheri a sweet smile, and she couldn't help smiling back. He was adorable, and Kade was just as good a father as she'd once dreamed he would be. Her own choices had crashed that fairytale castle around her ears.

She could hear him stomping into his boots in the entry then the sound of the door opening and closing. Grandma turned from the stove. "I can't even make porridge without water. Is there diesel in the generator, Chester?"

"Yup," grunted Grandpa. "He should figure it out all right. Seems like he knows his way around."

That was practically high praise.

"Doesn't mean you should be sneaking out to the stable to see him, missy." Grandpa's eyes bored into Cheri's. "Don't think to start up where you left off."

A flush crept up Cheri's cheeks. "I asked Grandma to watch Harmony for a few minutes. I didn't sneak out." She'd stayed in the stable so long after Kade had slammed out that Harmony had been asleep at the table, but at least Kade and Jericho had retired to their room. "Don't worry, we're not starting anything up. He's as disinterested as I am. We cleared the air a little, is all."

Grandpa grunted. "Those Delgados think they're something else. They bought out Archibalds, and young Trevor moved into the home place, as if one boy needs a four-thousand-square-foot house to himself. All of them's drivin' shiny new trucks like they struck gold."

A small house by Kade's parents' standards. They'd always been business-minded thinkers with long-term goals for setting up their three sons in the ranching business. That they'd tacked on Standing Rock Ranch shouldn't surprise her. It abutted Eaglecrest across River Road from Paradise Creek and stretched up into the mountain valleys. The Archibalds had leased out the land for summer grazing as far back as Cheri could remember.

"Why'd they sell out?"

"Michelle got tired of living out here in the sticks." Grandma scowled. "They bought an acreage south of Missoula where they could keep the horses. Stewy went back to lawyering."

No time like the present. Cheri took a deep breath. "You might want to consider selling, too. I was thinking I could get a job in Great Falls, maybe, and we could buy a little house together over there. A yard just big enough for a garden for you to putter in, Grandma. Less to take care of."

"We're not dead yet," muttered Grandpa. "'Sides, the ranch is yours."

"My ranching days are over." She'd lived with her grandparents from when she'd been Jericho's age, just a tot when her parents died in that accident. She'd ridden every inch of Paradise Creek Ranch and loved it all. The thought that Harmony wouldn't have similar memories stabbed her deep.

Grandpa wasn't done yet. "And we'd have to sell the horses. Cain't do that. They're friends."

They'd kept Blaze for her all these years. Would anyone want the old mare for their kids to learn on, or would she wind up in a glue factory?

"Not that Russ Delgado ain't offered to buy us out. Told him we're settin' right here until the good Lord calls us home." Grandpa's bushy eyebrows pulled together. "Then he had the nerve to ask if we was on speakin' terms with the good Lord."

"The man should mind his own business," muttered Grandma.

The two kids sat at the table, eyes wide, attention shifting between the adults as they spoke. Cheri surged to her feet. "Enough of that talk in front of little ears. I only want you to consider downsizing. Coming to live with Harmony and me." She gathered the dishes together.

"You move every five minutes," grunted Grandpa. "We're too old for that. Thought you had a good job and was gonna stay in Arcadia Valley and, next thing we know, you quit and come home."

"We've been meaning to ask what happened." Grandma leaned against the counter with her arms crossed.

A low hum filled the air, and the lights flickered then held. Kade the Perfect had saved the day. Again.

"I don't want to talk about it right now." Cheri jutted her chin toward her daughter and gave her grandmother a significant look.

Boots stomped on the porch boards outside before the

door creaked open. A minute later, Kade loomed in the doorway, his broad shoulders filling out the denim jacket. His gaze slid right over Cheri and settled on Grandpa. "It's running fine, Mr. Mackenzie, but it's nearly out of diesel. Got a full jerry can or two stashed somewhere? I'll top off the tank, and it should be good for a while."

Grandpa's head drooped. "Was gonna get more next trip to town. Cain't rightly lift the jug right now with them broken ribs."

"Feeling hale and hearty makes a big difference, doesn't it?" Kade nodded at Grandpa. "Be right back."

Cheri held her breath as he disappeared, the door thunking shut behind him.

"What's he gonna do now?" Grandma peered out the window above the kitchen sink. "Oh, no. We can't accept that boy's charity. He's pulling one of those big red jugs out of his truck box. Now he's taking it around back."

Grandpa stared at the table, scratching his head. "Don't see as we've got much choice at the moment. I'm sorry I cain't take good care of things myself right now, Edith. I'll pay the boy back. Don't worry."

If Kade's motivation was to kill her grandparents with kindness, he was certainly succeeding.

CHAPTER 4

K ade hated leaving his son inside with the Mackenzies, but he'd be safer in there than outside. Jericho would be fine. He seemed to adore Harmony, but he'd get over it when contact was cut. Which would be soon.

The axe sliced through another log with a resounding crack. Kade could only be thankful for a task that required his concentration and worked up a sweat at the same time. What would he do when he'd split and stacked all the wood? He could tighten the loose hinge he'd noticed on the generator lean-to, but he didn't have rubber washers to tackle the bathroom tap.

Cra-ack.

He tossed the halves aside and reached for another log. The whine of a distant snowmobile cut through the snow-muffled stillness. He paused and tilted his head to one side, listening. Sounded like Trevor's Polaris. It would be just like his big brother to come searching for him.

Kade doubled his effort. He was close enough to the end of the scattered heap of logs — at least what he could find in the knee-deep snow — that he wanted to complete the job. He tried to push aside the faint hope that Cheri might be watching out the window, regretting her fling with Dillon when she saw Kade's hard work. Instead, she probably realized he was a coward trying to avoid her.

The snowmobile grew louder, roaring into the yard when Kade was down to the last dozen logs.

Trevor swung off his machine in the sudden silence. "Bro! Glad you're okay. Mom sent me looking for you." He sauntered over, shooting a glance at the log house, then lowered his voice. "Must have been some desperation to send you here. You should've stayed in town and sent a message."

Kade set the axe head on the chopping block and leaned on the handle. "It's worse than that."

Trevor's eyebrows shot up as he tugged off his helmet. "Cheri's here."

Sympathy slid over his brother's face. "No way."

"And she has a six-year-old."

Trevor blinked then blinked again before running his hands through his sweaty, already tousled hair. "So that's why..." His words drifted away as he shook his head.

"Looks like."

"I'm sorry, bro. Where's Jer?"

"In the house with them. I couldn't very well have him out here while I was chopping wood. Chester's got some busted ribs."

Trevor glanced at the battlefield of strewn split logs. "I'll stack 'em. Then we'll grab Jer and head up to Eaglecrest. It might be a day or two before they get that avalanche cleared. Maybe not until after Thanksgiving. River Road isn't the only one hit by the storm from what we heard on the scanner."

Kade reached for another log. "Can we get the tractor down there and clear it ourselves?"

Trevor gathered split wood and stacked it under the porch overhang. "Big job. It's full of downed trees covering over thirty feet of road."

"Nothing a couple of chainsaws and a front loader can't handle."

"You haven't seen the mess."

Kade grunted and sliced through another log. It was a public road, even though only Delgado land lay beyond the slide. Just, leaving his truck at Paradise Creek meant he had to see Cheri again when he retrieved it. He preferred ripping off adhesive bandages and getting the pain over with at once.

Any other logs would have to be discovered after the snow melted. Kade laid the axe in the top of his truck toolbox and helped Trevor stack.

"Stealing Chester's tools?"

"As if. I got mine out. His needs sharpening." Kade glanced toward the window, but no one peered out. He lowered his voice anyway. "Whole place is rundown, really."

"Chester should've accepted Dad's offer."

Kade wondered why the old man hadn't. Pride, probably. And maybe holding out for Cheri's return. All Kade knew was he wasn't going to be the one moving down to Paradise Creek to secure the holding for his father, like Trevor had done on the Archibald place. He'd told his parents that. Dad had only nodded.

"How'd the Cowboy Santa meeting go? Sorry I missed it, but maybe it's just as well, or we'd both have been stranded."

He could assign the Mackenzies to Trevor. No one would blame him for trading them off, but the thought of his older brother hanging around Cheri didn't sit well, either.

Why, Delgado, you're jealous.

Yes. Yes, he was. Jealous that someone had stolen his bride and left her with a child. Kade should have been the father of her children. She should have been the mother of his. His thoughts flashed to Daniela. He'd done his best by her in the brief time they'd had. At least she hadn't expected him to love her completely.

"Bro?"

Kade kicked a log out of the snow then tossed it at Trevor. "James is emailing the assignments. I didn't see who he gave you."

"Better not be here." Trevor stacked the last few pieces of firewood, cut side down. "Not for you, either."

"I agreed before I knew Cheri was back. Figured it was time to get over the past and let Jesus' love do some talking."

Trevor snorted. "Good idea in theory."

Kade couldn't think of a single reply. "I'll get Jer and meet you back out here."

A HEADACHE like no other pulsed in Cheri's skull. It had been a mistake returning to Saddle Springs, but where she should have gone instead eluded her. Anywhere but here, where Kade's adorable little boy scribbled across a paper with a blue crayon then eyed the careful artwork Harmony hunched over beside him at the table. Where her grandparents, one with clicking knitting needles, radiated disapproval from their rockers on either side of the kitchen wood stove. Where the sharp crack of Kade's axe resounded rhythmically just outside.

If only Dillon hadn't found her. She'd been happy in Arcadia Valley. She'd made friends and even begun attending church again. Had a decent job at a daycare where she could be near Harmony. She'd cautiously begun to hope that her nightmare years were behind her.

Cheri rubbed her temples. What was she going to do? How long would it take Dillon to arrive? She'd led him straight back to where it all began when she should have made a beeline for someplace safer, like Kansas. Or Maine.

Jericho slid off the chair, ran over to her, and smiled up winsomely. "I stinky."

Wow, he wasn't kidding. Should she change him or leave him for his dad? Who knew how much longer Kade would be? It was practically child abuse to leave the little guy the way he was. Cheri rose from her seat and held out her hand. "Come on. Show me where your diapers are."

His little fingers gripped hers, and her heart flipped over. Jericho pushed open the door to the room where he and his dad had spent the night. The bed was neatly made with Kade's few things lined up in a row at the foot.

Cheri closed her eyes and tried to inhale the essence of Kade, but all she got was the essence of Jericho. She tugged a diaper from the box, took the child to the bathroom, and completed the task. Then, unable to resist any longer, she lifted the boy into her arms.

Jericho's little arms squeezed her neck. "Tanku."

Her heart swelled as she hugged him back. "You're welcome. You're such a sweet little guy, aren't you?"

He nodded. "Jer'cho sweet."

She nuzzled him. "You have a good daddy, huh?"

"Daddy good."

Yeah, she knew. She'd never had a doubt. She buried her nose in the little boy's neck. *Lord, if You've truly forgiven me, help me make things right.* Of course, just last night she'd said horrible things to Kade, bitter words that had kept her awake half the night. How many new things would God have to forgive her for every day? She was such a mess. Surely God had a limit to His mercy.

Last Easter she'd sat beside her friends in church, marveling at God's wide, amazing love. Today, she imagined Him in a rocker in the kitchen, shaking His head with accusing eyes and pursed lips.

She carried Jericho toward the kitchen. As they passed through the entry, the door swung open and Kade's dark eyes snapped to meet hers. She loosened her grip on the little boy, but he still clung to her neck. What must Kade be thinking?

Cheri cleared her throat. "Just changed his diaper." She disengaged Jericho's arms and set him on the floor. "He smells a lot better now."

Jericho dashed across the stone pavers and tripped but, before he landed, his daddy scooped him up.

If only God had caught her like that before she'd skinned her knees... and worse. She barely remembered her own father. Had he been as kind and sweet as Kade Delgado? Would growing up with a loving daddy have given her the security — taught her the wisdom — to resist Dillon Scarborough? Looking back, Dillon had played her skillfully, and her needy heart had yearned for that bit of excitement before settling down to a predictable life as Kade's bride. How foolish she had been.

Trevor Delgado shut the door behind himself and Kade. Now the piercing gaze of two Delgado men riveted her. She forced herself to breathe. "Hi, Trevor."

He reached as though to tip a cowboy hat that wasn't there. "Cheri."

"How'd you get through?"

"Snowmobile. Come to take Kade and Jericho up to Eaglecrest. We'll get his truck when the road's open."

Jericho gripped Kade's cheeks between his little hands and peered into his daddy's eyes. "Snow'bile?"

"You got it, bucko."

"Get boots." The child pointed and kicked gently.

Kade set him down, and his gaze swung straight back to Cheri. "I'll leave the groceries for you and your grandparents. It's not like I can take them on the snowmobile anyway, and there's no point in them going to waste."

"I'll pay you for them."

He dipped his chin. "It's okay to accept a gift."

But not from Kade Delgado. Not when he'd offered her everything, himself included, and she'd basically thumbed her nose.

Kade toed off his boots. "I'll get what I can carry and say goodbye to your grandparents."

She stepped aside and let him pass. He returned with the box of diapers stuffed into the baby carrier, set it down, then walked through to the kitchen. Meanwhile, Trevor helped Jericho with his jacket then straightened.

"I don't know why you're back, Cheri Mackenzie, but don't mess with my brother."

Strange how Kade wasn't the only Delgado suspicious of her motives. She straightened her shoulders. "Not planning on it, Trevor."

He assessed her. "I mean it."

Something akin to hope tried to bubble up. Didn't it mean something if Trevor thought his brother might fall for her again? But — oh, yeah — she'd made sure that would never happen with the caustic words she'd fired at him last night. "Point taken."

Kade brushed past her, yanked his boots back on, hoisted the carrier to his back, and followed Trevor and Jericho out the door without another word to her.

Cheri moved to the sidelight and watched him settle

Jericho between his knees. Trevor started the engine, and the snowmobile swept a wake of snow as it turned and roared up the driveway.

Silence. Emptiness.

She stared into the cold, white expanse beyond the porch.

"Cheri?"

Grandma wouldn't let her wallow. With a sigh, Cheri returned to the kitchen. "Do you want me to fix some lunch? Or maybe you'd like more coffee." The old enamel percolator sat on the wood stove, keeping warm.

"Good thing he's gone." Grandma looked up from her knitting, but her fingers kept moving.

Grandpa shifted, and a wince crossed his face. "Big help, though. Got enough wood split for a week at least."

"And enough groceries until we can get to town again."

Cheri forced out a smile. "That's great."

"Left me the keys to that fandangled truck of his. Never drove one of them before."

"And you're not going to now, Chester. It was just polite on his part, being as he had to leave it here. Why, we might need to move it to plow out the... yard." Grandma's voice faded.

Right. Who was going to do that? Not Cheri. More than Kade's truck would be in danger if she tried to fire up the old John Deere and searched her memory on how to use the blade. Why had she been so brash to think she could actually help her grandparents? Sure, she could feed three horses, but splitting logs like Kade had done would require a week's recovery in a bubble bath in the claw foot tub. By then they'd be long out of firewood again.

No, her only hope was to convince them to leave the ranch behind, even if only to rent a little house in Saddle Springs over the winter. Would that slow Dillon down any? Not likely.

Cheri crossed the kitchen to put on water for tea, but her attention snagged on Harmony's drawing.

Her daughter looked up at her with a wistful expression. On the paper stood a woman and a child, both with flowing yellow hair, Harmony's trademark rendition of Cheri and herself. Beside them stood a man and a little boy, each with something suspiciously like a cowboy hat on their heads. Harmony wanted to be part of a family, and it looked like she'd decided Kade and Jericho would be a perfect fit.

Not gonna happen, sweetheart. But she couldn't say the words aloud. She squeezed Harmony's shoulder and offered a smile before turning back for the kettle.

Only thing was, had Kade seen the drawing?

CHAPTER 5

H ow does her return make you feel?"

Trust Mom to get right to the heart of the matter. Kade shook the giant pan of popping corn over the propane kitchen stove and listened to a few kernels explode. "I'm not sure." He'd been doing his best to steel himself against Cheri until he'd seen Harmony's drawing. She'd looked up at him with sad eyes when he'd said goodbye. The message had been clear.

In the other room, his brother Sawyer lay on the floor setting up the toy ranch while Jericho made neighing sounds and ran circles around his uncle. Both Kade's brothers needed a woman in their lives. To start a family. Kade had had his chance. Two of them, really, and failed at both.

He glanced at his mother, who melted butter on the other burner. In her mid-fifties, his mom looked pretty good, active and trim for a woman who oversaw Eaglecrest's entire operations from her office in the large ranch home.

"I thought I was over her," he confessed.

Mom smiled and shook her head.

"Okay, I tried to be." For Daniela's sake. For his sanity's sake. And for Jericho's sake.

"Maybe God brought her back for a reason."

Kade snorted. "To remind me I'm a failure? Because Cheri definitely has no interest in me. She made that pretty clear."

Mom raised her eyebrows then turned the flame off under the melted butter.

"And it's mutual," he hurried on. "What she did to me is unforgivable. And with Dillon Scarborough, of all people." The jerk was a weasel. What had Cheri ever seen in him? While wearing Kade's diamond on her finger, no less.

"I'm not making light of the situation, son. I'm also not suggesting you try to win her again. We've done much worse things to God, and He stands ready to forgive us if we only ask Him. He wipes us clean, as white as the two feet of snow that's fallen since yesterday."

The pan grated against the element as Kade shook it, corn popping in an ever-increasing staccato that eventually faded. He flicked off the knob and looked down at his mother. "God's motive for that kind of forgiveness is to shower love on us and win us back."

"The ultimate romance." Mom slid her arm around his waist and gave him a squeeze. "Not every form of forgiveness can — or even should — have that much attached to it. But, if you can come to peace over Cheri, it will free your heart to love again. Jericho needs a woman in his life, and so do you."

"We're fine. We've got you and Ruthie and Elnora." Kade dumped the popcorn into a huge bowl and reached for a large spoon while Mom drizzled on the butter. He stirred as she added salt, pepper, and a good dose of nutritional yeast. He inhaled the homey aroma.

Mom nibbled a kernel. "Perfect."

He lifted the bowl and turned toward the great room, but Mom's hand on his arm stopped him. "A grandmother and some hired help are no replacement for a loving mommy in a little boy's life. You're right that we are filling in for Daniela and that we all love Jericho. I don't begrudge Ruthie having Jericho on a chair helping her cook, or Elnora keeping an eye on him while she folds laundry and cleans, but it's not the same thing."

Kade grimaced. "Getting married just to supply a mother for my son doesn't seem right. I want to love again. I even thought maybe I was ready to." Prodded by Lauren Yanovich, a childhood friend, he'd actually started looking around at church, which had led to realizing the needs of the single moms in town, which had led to Cowboy Santa. Which, in a surprising twist, had led straight back to Cheri Mackenzie.

"Sometimes love follows, son. True love, the kind the Father has for us, is action-based, not feelings-based. We make a decision to love someone and then follow through."

Hadn't he done that with Daniela? He'd known it

wouldn't be a bed of roses, not when she'd told him her full story. But, what she'd asked of him, he'd been willing to give. If she'd beat the odds and lived, mutual respect would surely have grown into love, but it was never meant to be. Now she was gone.

And Cheri Mackenzie was back at Paradise Creek.

"CAN I HAVE A PONY?" Harmony climbed the metal gate of Blaze's stall and held her hand steady as the mare nuzzled it.

"We're not going to stay at the ranch." Cheri adjusted the glow of the kerosene lantern hanging on a peg. The thought of an open flame in a stable filled with hay and horses made her twitch, but she had little choice. This had been Grandpa's backup light source out here as long as she could remember.

Harmony turned, her blue eyes narrowing. "But you said..."

"I know what I said." That had been on the long drive north to Montana. Before she'd trudged into Java Springs and laid eyes on Kade Delgado after six and a half years. "But things have changed."

The little girl's lips poked out a pout. "You always say that."

Cheri tried for a breezy tone. "We stayed in Arcadia Valley a long time. A year and a half."

"When are we going back? I miss my friends."

She squeezed her daughter. "I know. I miss mine, too." The people at work. The people at church. Even her neighbors. But she couldn't stay after Dillon had located them. He'd threatened once to take Harmony away from her, but it wasn't because he loved the child they'd created. It was only a power trip — one that would work, because Cheri would be right where he wanted her, under his grinding thumb.

Not gonna happen. Not if she had to move every six months until Harmony had grown up. Paradise Creek Ranch wasn't safe. Grandpa was too old to protect her.

Kade wasn't.

Kade was leaner, wirier, and four inches taller than Dillon. He could send the scum flying with one swift punch. It would be satisfying to watch, actually.

"But, Mama, I *want* a pony."

If Kade were Harmony's father, she'd have a pony, a puppy, and a safe, secure life. They'd have built their dream house on the edge of Delgado land, overlooking Paradise Creek. She and Harmony would never have wanted for anything. Of course, she wouldn't have Harmony. Kade wouldn't have Jericho, but they'd have had other children by now.

So many regrets.

"Mama?"

She brushed her little girl's hair out of her eyes. "Sorry, honey." They'd stay until the New Year, if Dillon didn't find them first. She'd look for a small place in town for her grandparents, somewhere with caring neighbors nearby, and then she'd take Harmony and head out again. She had friends in Michigan. Maybe that would throw Dillon off for a year or two.

"As soon as the snowplow has been up the road, Grandpa will drive us to town to get our car. Won't that be nice?" She'd left a message on the tow truck company's voicemail where to find her.

Harmony turned away with a frown.

Right, the child had no attachment to the car. Neither did Cheri. She'd dumped vehicles as often as she'd switched wigs and addresses.

The sound of the sliding stable door caused her to whirl, but it was only Grandpa stomping in, kicking the snow off his boots. His eyes snapped right to hers. "Thought I might find you out here."

"Does Grandma need my help inside?"

He shook his head as he crossed the worn floor to the stall next to Blaze's. Barney nickered softly and stretched over the rail. "Hey, old fella," crooned Grandpa.

Harmony leaned closer. "Is that your horse, Grandpa?"

"Sure is. Barney's been with me a long time."

Cheri's heart caught at the wistfulness in his voice. When was the last time he'd sat astride? Why couldn't he see it was time to move into town? Hanging on at his age only forced a focus on the past. "I fed all three. I'll muck out the stalls this afternoon. They might like a bit of time in the corral now that the wind has died down."

"Snow's too deep. It drifts in there." His gnarled hands caressed Barney's head. "Been wanting to talk to you."

Her gut tightened. "Not with Harmony."

Grandpa jerked his chin toward the little girl. "Run along to your grandmother."

Cheri wanted to protest, to put it off, but could come up with no good excuse. She lifted Harmony down. "Stay on the path back to the house." She slid the stable door open.

Harmony stuck out her lower lip. "But I want to pet the horses some more."

"Later. There'll be plenty of chances."

"But you said—"

Cheri laid her finger over her daughter's lips. "I promise. Now off you go."

Harmony scowled at her then trudged away, kicking at the snow.

That's how Cheri felt, too. If only she could indulge in a temper tantrum herself. Life was so unfair, and Grandpa wasn't likely to be the most understanding or sensitive. She stood and watched until her daughter pushed open the door to the log house before turning back. The familiar prayer washed through her mind, the desperation in it long since given over to quiet dread. *Lord, please, please help me. Or at least keep Harmony safe.*

"What did you want to talk about?"

"Shut the door and have a seat." Grandpa pointed at a bale.

She did, then folded her hands in her lap. The low hiss of the kerosene lantern was punctuated by the horses shifting around their stalls. Any other noises that might exist in the universe were muffled by the thick cocoon of snow. The stillness should be comforting, but not with her nerves strung tight.

"Your grandma ain't doing so well."

Cheri's head jerked upright. Of all the things she thought he'd lead off with, this wasn't one of them. "What's wrong?" Arthritis? Cancer? Dementia?

"Her ticker."

Surely they'd have told her if Grandma'd had a heart attack. "How bad?"

Grandpa rubbed Barney's shoulder. "She's had some episodes. Doc's a mite concerned."

"Episodes?" Her mind bounced from arrhythmia to pacemakers to quadruple bypass. "What is he going to do about it? Has Grandma seen a specialist?"

"We're thinkin' on it."

She couldn't sit still any longer but surged to her feet. "What's there to think about? Grandma's not that old." What, late seventies? Cheri couldn't remember their birth years at the moment, not with her mind leaping. "Is it money? I can help." How, she had no idea, but there had to be a way. Just as a rolling stone gathered no moss, so a single mother moving and switching jobs every year or two didn't collect much in savings. But she owed her grandparents everything. They'd taken her in, fed her, cared for her without a single complaint. Sure, they weren't the demonstrative sort, but she'd never doubted their love.

Her grandfather shook his head. "We'll be okay."

"Sell the ranch."

He pierced her with his eyes. "We cain't. That's one of the things we need to talk about, you'n me."

Cheri gathered her hair in both hands and flipped it over her shoulder. "Of course, you can. It's time."

Grandpa pointed at the bale, but she ignored his silent command. Instead, she braced her feet and set her hands on her hips. Just like she'd done last night when it was Kade who faced her in the stable.

"Paradise Creek ain't ours, missy. It's yours."

"No, it's yours. There's no need to hold it for me. I won't be moving back." Yes, she'd dreamed of the day she could offer Paradise Creek to Kade, almost like a dowry. There was no one else to inherit. Her father had been an only child, as was she. But she'd never been in a hurry for her name on the deed. How could she be, with how much her grandparents meant to her? If they could live forever, right here, she'd be happy. But not when they couldn't keep the place up. Not when they were in pain. "Sell it."

"You ain't listening."

She searched his weathered face. "You're not explaining."

"Your folks bought Paradise Creek. Gave us a home when we was down on our luck. Then when they passed on, you were the heir, not us. Shoulda told you long ago. Didn't think of it that you might not know until the other day. We been takin' care of it for you." He looked around with a grimace. "Ain't done such a great job. Sorry."

Cheri's mind reeled, and her body teetered. Now

sitting on the bale seemed the best plan, after all. "This is a terrible April Fool's joke, Grandpa."

"Ain't April, and ain't no joke."

"I don't understand."

"There's nothing to not understand." Grandpa waved his hand. "This is yours. All of it. We've got a bit set by, Edith and me. We'll be fine."

A thousand thoughts stampeded through her brain, but only one stood out. "You said Delgados wanted to buy? Then I'll sell it and get Grandma the care she needs."

"Don't do that, missy. Your folks wouldn't want that for you. It's your heritage."

Her heritage? Right next door to the man she'd pledged to marry and then cheated on? Right next door to the best and worst memories of her entire life? Right in plain sight where Dillon Scarborough could find their daughter any time he chose?

She shook her head. She just needed to see the papers and confirm that her grandfather wasn't in late stages of dementia, that her name really was on the deed of Paradise Creek Ranch.

And then she'd get rid of it.

CHAPTER 6

Okay, there are lots of potatoes, and you took the chicken out of the freezer last night." Not that it was completely thawed, as cold as the kitchen got overnight. Cheri tapped a pen against the table as she tried to figure out how to create anything resembling Thanksgiving dinner. Would her grandparents have celebrated if she and Harmony had stayed in Arcadia Valley? Didn't look like it.

Grandma opened a cupboard and shuffled several packages and cans. "There's stuffing mix here. Candied sweet potatoes."

Cheri managed not to flinch. She and Harmony had been invited to a lavish feast at the home of friends in Arcadia Valley. Joanna had bought a free-range turkey from a nearby farm, and the gang had divvied up the remainder of the menu of fresh, locally grown food. Cheri had offered to bring the creamed spinach, since the cooling weather had brought the various greens to robust health in the greenhouse at work. Hopefully someone else picked up the slack when she bailed out at the last minute.

A faint sound grew louder. It almost sounded like the jangle of harnesses, but it couldn't be. Yet, when a horse snorted outside, Cheri's pulse sped up.

Grandma leaned over the kitchen sink and peered out. "What on earth...?"

"Who's there? What's going on?" Surely she'd kept her voice casual.

"That woman."

Not Kade, then. But why would it be?

Footsteps on the deck. Then a knock at the door. Grandma pinned Cheri with a look. "I'll get it."

Certainly she would, but that wouldn't keep Cheri from following. Cheri slipped into the doorway as Grandma opened the door a crack. "Yes?"

Oh, man. Why was her grandmother so ungracious?

"Happy Thanksgiving, Edith!" Gloria Delgado's voice was cheerful and friendly.

"And to you." Grandma didn't invite the neighbor in.

"I was just thinking how this storm came in out of nowhere and River Road hasn't been plowed out yet. It likely caught you unprepared, what with Chester's accident and all."

Grandma mumbled something noncommittal.

"We'd invited the Carmichael family to have Thanksgiving dinner with us, but of course they can't get up our road. We have so much food it will take a week to eat it all." Gloria laughed merrily. "So I told Russ to harness up the sleigh, and I'd come down and fetch your family if you didn't have big plans."

"Thanks, but we're fine." Grandma started to shut the door.

Wouldn't this give Cheri the perfect opportunity to talk to Kade's parents about buying Paradise Creek? The sooner she got the ranch off her hands, the sooner she could get her grandparents settled somewhere else. She stepped forward. "Good morning, Gloria."

Grandma glared at her, but Cheri tugged the door out of her hands.

The other woman turned back with a pleasant smile. "Why, hello, Cheri."

There should be frost in Kade's mother's voice, but Cheri couldn't detect it. "That's a very generous offer you made."

Gloria's eyes lit up. "I meant it."

"You're right that we don't have much planned. My grandparents weren't expecting my daughter and me until the last minute, and they hadn't been to town for supplies in a couple of weeks."

Gloria pointed to the pair of horses behind her, hitched to the sleigh that had been in the Delgado family for over a century. "I'm here to take you home with me. One of the boys will be happy to bring you back after dinner."

They'd be happy to get rid of the Mackenzies again, all right. The warning in Trevor's voice yesterday hadn't been lost on Cheri. She braced herself. "We'd love to come. Wouldn't we, Grandma?"

Her grandmother mumbled something about not feeling so good, and Harmony's voice came from behind them. "Horses!" The little girl elbowed past and stood on the doorstep, hair flying everywhere, staring at the scene before her with wide eyes.

"Gloria, this is my daughter, Harmony. Honey, this lady is Mrs. Delgado, Mr. Kade's mom."

"She's beautiful. She looks just like you."

Why was Gloria here, being so sweet? But she'd never been anything but kind. And what was the appropriate response? "Thank you. She's a good kid." A kid who didn't deserve the life she'd gotten. But, then, who did? What had Cheri done wrong as a child to deserve the deaths of her parents, being raised by grandparents who rarely smiled... and then Dillon?

Harmony looked up at Kade's mom. "Are those your horses? They're bee-*yoo*-tiful."

"They are, aren't they?" Gloria crouched beside Harmony. "The one closest to us is Tuck, and the other one is Nip." She raised her eyebrows as she looked back to Cheri.

Nip and Tuck. The same Percheron horses they'd had in those long-ago days. Cheri had ridden in that sleigh a dozen times at least, tucked at Kade's side, flying over the snow. She'd given up so much in that fleeting time with Dillon. Like Eve in the garden, Cheri had known instantly that she'd made the wrong choice, no matter how appealing it had seemed in the moment.

"Would you like to ride in that sleigh, honey? Mrs.

Delgado invited us for Thanksgiving dinner. You'd get to see Jericho again."

Harmony did a little jiggle dance on the threshold. "Yes, please!"

Grandma snorted. "I don't think—"

Cheri put her hand on her grandmother's arm. "I think we should. Won't you come in for a minute, Mrs. Delgado? It won't take long for us to get ready." She'd send Grandma to warn Grandpa, but then it would be two against one.

"You're making a mistake, missy," Grandma huffed under her breath, as Cheri guided her back inside.

"Do you still have that royal blue sweater, Grandma? It looks so good on you. Brings out the color of your eyes."

Grandma sent a scowl over her shoulder at Gloria Delgado then stomped off down the hallway. That left her grandfather.

Cheri led the way into the kitchen. "Hey, Grandpa! Look who's here. Gloria Delgado has invited us to Thanksgiving dinner. She even brought the sleigh down to give us a ride." Cheri bustled over to the counter and tucked the chicken back in the fridge. It'd thaw more slowly and be fine until tomorrow or even the next day. "Isn't that nice of her?"

He looked up from the latest copy of Working Ranch magazine.

"Howdy, neighbor!" Gloria reached out to shake his hand. "I hope your ribs are healing up well."

At least he accepted the handshake. "I'm fine." He narrowed his gaze at Cheri. "What's going on?"

She smiled at him. "You heard me. Let's not keep her waiting."

Harmony tugged at her hand. "Can I wear my new dress?"

The soft, plush dress Cheri had bought her daughter for the upcoming Christmas season. Things had sure changed. "No, honey. Wear pants so you can play outside with Jericho. Plus, it will be cold in the sleigh, so put on your snowsuit."

That lower lip came out. "But—"

"Please listen." And that went double for Grandpa.

He heaved to his feet, wincing as he did. "This ain't such a grand idea," he mumbled as he shuffled out.

Marriage must be easier when a couple agreed on things. At least her grandparents were united on this one, but Cheri wasn't giving in. "It's a great idea. The Delgados are only being neighborly, and I think it's really nice of them." She turned to Gloria. "Would you mind waiting a minute? I need to get changed, too. Please have a seat. I can pour you a coffee if you like?"

Gloria smiled. "Take your time. I'll wait here." She settled onto a chair at the table and laid her gloves down.

Cheri scurried to her bedroom and flung open her suitcase. She hadn't even bothered to unpack yet. What should she wear? What was pretty but not wrinkled? She shook out a baby blue knit. The soft fuzz covered the effects of a few days jammed in a tight space. Plus, it looked good on her.

She wasn't wearing it so Kade's eyes would be drawn to her. Not at all. More that she needed confidence, and wearing something she felt attractive in would help. She'd be stupid to wear an old flannel shirt, right? Right. She slipped on the sweater along with her newest skinny jeans then eyeballed herself in the mirror. A little mascara wouldn't hurt. Lipstick. A pretty hair clip.

Definitely none of the primping was so Kade would regret his dismissal of her the other evening. But she'd been the one to ruin the promise of everything in front of her.

KADE SQUIRMED UNEASILY in his chair as Dad rose at the head of the Thanksgiving table. Norman Rockwell could have painted this scene, which begged the question, had everything been as idyllic as it looked in that old artwork, or were there undercurrents of tension not painted on people's faces?

"Today is a day of giving thanks to God for His many blessings to us." Dad's gaze lingered on the Mackenzie quartet gathered around the far end of the table. "Our custom is to go around the circle, and each person says something they are thankful for this holiday season. Why don't you go first, Trevor, and we'll take this clockwise."

"I'm thankful we got all the cattle down from the high ranges before that crazy snowstorm."

"Kade?"

His mind raced. He'd mention Jericho, but his family

would jump on that answer, since they didn't allow repeats from the previous year. "I'm thankful for electricity... and that we can manage even without it." He nudged his young son. "What are you thankful for, bucko?"

Jericho peered down the table, his face in a wide grin. "Ha'mony!"

A few people chuckled, but it sounded strained. Soon, Dad got around to Cheri's grandfather at the foot of the table. "Chester? How about you?"

The old man stared hard at Dad. "Grateful my girl is home again."

Dad nodded. "Cheri?"

Man, that blue sweater looked good on her. Her blond hair was clipped to the side and flowed over one shoulder. Kade had managed to keep from focusing on his former fiancée until this moment. She looked amazing.

"I'm thankful for God's forgiveness, and that He gives second chances."

Kade almost missed the quick glance she sent his way. He could do forgiveness and second chances, too. But, no. She'd told him in no uncertain terms that she was no longer interested in him. Ever-present regrets swarmed his emotions. If only the heartache could be erased, the empty years deleted.

"Harmony, what are you thankful for?"

The little girl bounced in her chair, her eyes bright. "Horses and sleigh rides!"

Cheri looked down, biting her lip, as many around the table laughed.

Kade couldn't take his eyes off her. What was she thinking? She'd been the most horse-crazy girl around when they were young. He thought he'd known her so well, but he hadn't. Had he imagined her love for horses like he obviously had her love for him? His heart ached anew. No. Both had been real. True. Beautiful. How had Dillon managed to steal her away and, with her, Kade's future?

Guilt nudged in. Daniela had given him Jericho, and he couldn't imagine a life without his precious young son. Paths had diverged that fateful day, and Kade had somehow kept living. Found a measure of happiness — or peace, at least — but the wounds had never completely healed. Maybe if Cheri had actually broken up with him instead of vanishing. Maybe if he'd been the one to break things off... but he never would have. He'd loved her with all the focus and passion a twenty-two-year-old could muster, and that had been a lot. Oceans wide and mountains high.

She peeked at him again, and this time their gazes held.

He could love her again. He'd never really stopped.

"...IN JESUS' name, amen."

With a start, Cheri realized the circle had continued and Kade's father had asked the blessing on their dinner. The Delgado cook, Ruthie, placed a huge golden turkey in front of Russ, and he began to carve. Chatter picked up as steaming bowls of garlic mashed potatoes, creamy green bean casserole, and aromatic dressing began to make their rounds. She watched Kade put a healthy scoop of everything on his plate and add a dollop to his son's. A good daddy. She'd always known he would be.

Her heart pinched with loss. Yes, she was ever so thankful for God's forgiveness, which had made all the difference when she'd stopped running from it, but she wanted Kade's, too. If only she could rewind the clock and flip back the calendar pages, but that could never happen. She'd come to the stable the other evening to ask his forgiveness, and he'd told her he didn't need her anymore. If only she'd begged instead of mouthing off things she didn't mean. It had been her pride, not her heart, retaliating against the rejection.

The food looked and smelled amazing, reminding her of the feast her friends would be enjoying today back in Arcadia Valley. Just like them, Kade's mom had always had a large garden and focused on homegrown food. The greenhouse Russ had built for her ten years or so ago had extended the growing season deep in the Bitterroots.

Too bad Cheri could barely get a mouthful down. The problem wasn't just Kade's presence, although that was a lot of it. She just needed to get through this meal and wait for the first opportunity to ask Russ if she could talk to him for a few minutes. How she'd get him aside without her grandparents or the entire Delgado family listening in, she had no idea, but she had to. Life would be so much easier if he'd just buy Paradise Creek and she didn't have to call in a real estate agent.

Because Paul Scarborough owned Saddle Springs Realty, and it would be impossible to hide her ownership of the ranch from him. She'd rather Dillon's dad didn't even find out she was back in the area, but the owner of even a rundown spread like Paradise Creek? There'd be no way he'd keep that news to himself.

CHAPTER 7

Good job on the turkey, Dad." Trevor leaned back in his chair, patting his stomach. "I wouldn't have thought of using the barbecue as an oven."

Russ Delgado grinned at his son. "I've made a few trips around the sun, cowboy. This was not my first rodeo."

The few morsels Cheri had managed to eat had indeed been delectable, and Harmony had put a surprising amount away. Was the child headed for another growth spurt? Keeping her in clothes was enough of a challenge as it was.

Gloria smiled at Cheri. "We're so glad you joined us."

Cheri managed a smile in return. Her grandparents had been slightly south of gracious, as though reminded of what age and inability was stealing from them. "Thank you for the invitation. The pumpkin pie was especially delicious."

"Why, thanks, honey. Russ and I made those last evening, and Ruthie and Elnora prepared everything else. Ruthie's got some great recipes up her sleeve. We're so blessed to have her. Both of them, truly. And isn't it amazing what you can do without electricity?"

Kade's mom was so gracious, deflecting attention to others.

The youngest Delgado brother leaned in. "You baked those in the grill, too, Dad?"

"Sure did. A barbecue isn't just for steak, son."

She could have been part of this family. Instead, she'd blown her chances and escaped to Reno with Dillon, and a woman named Daniela had taken her place. Cheri shot a quick glance at Kade as he leaned close to Jericho, his arm around the boy's chair, listening to whatever the two-year-old whispered in his ear. Had Kade loved Daniela? Like, really loved her, the way he'd loved Cheri? She couldn't imagine him marrying someone he didn't love, even on the rebound.

He whispered something in return, mussed Jericho's hair, then glanced up. His gaze snagged on Cheri's, and she forgot to breathe. The intensity of those eyes had always held the power to drive her to her knees.

Trevor, Sawyer, and their dad hooted at something Cheri had missed, and Kade turned away.

Grandma nudged her. "Anytime they want to take us home, I'm ready."

No. Not before Cheri'd had a chance to talk to Russ. Wanting to watch Kade had nothing to do with her desire to stay a little longer. "I think it would be rude to ask for that right after dinner, don't you?" she whispered back.

Grandma shrugged. "We can blame your grandfather and say he's not feeling well."

Grandpa looked fine. It was Grandma who'd been out of sorts and low on energy.

Cheri stood and gathered a few plates together. "Let me give you a hand with cleaning up before you take us back to Paradise Creek."

Russ waved his hand. "No, no. You're our guest. Ruthie and Elnora will handle everything." He grimaced as the grandfather clock struck two. "Guess we're not watching the Cowboys play today. That's the worst thing about having no power on Thanksgiving."

Gloria swatted his arm. "Men and football. I'll never understand the allure."

"Maybe we need to start a new tradition," Russ said. "Do we have any board games that work well for eight people?"

"No way, Dad." Trevor groaned. "Have we prayed for a miracle yet? The kind where the power magically flips on right about... now?" He snapped his fingers and looked up at the chandelier expectantly.

Cheri couldn't help chuckling along with the others. But, still, games? Not how she wanted to spend the remainder of the day.

Ruthie rolled in a small trolley and began stacking dishes onto it. The middle-aged widow had been ensconced at Eaglecrest as long as Cheri could remember.

"Not much of one for games," Grandpa announced. "If it's all the same to you."

"Sure, no problem, Chester." Russ rose to his feet. "Shall we retire to the great room?"

"And stare at the blank black box on the wall?" teased Sawyer, elbowing his older brother.

Trevor dug back. "We could go out and check on that heifer."

"Now there's an idea." The brothers excused themselves and strode down the hallway, boots clicking on the wooden floorboards.

Russ lifted Jericho from his booster, tucked the squealing child under his arm like a football, and went into the other room.

Cheri surged to her feet. This moment of transition might be what she'd been waiting for.

Grandpa braced his hands on the table and pulled himself upright. He stared at Cheri. "Are you ready...?"

"Soon." She gave him a quick grin and reached for Harmony's hand. "Want to play with Jericho a few more minutes?"

"Yes!"

Cheri led her daughter into the great room. She probably had less than a minute before someone else came in. Someone like Kade, or even Grandpa. She needed to talk quickly. "Russ? I have a question for you." She glanced over her shoulder, but the coast was still clear.

"Cheri. What can I help you with?"

Why did Kade's parents have to be so nice? If only he'd follow through one last time. "My grandfather told me you'd offered to buy Paradise Creek a while back. It is now for sale."

The older man's eyebrows hiked up. "Doesn't Chester feel he can talk to me himself?"

She took a deep breath. "The thing is, my grandparents don't own the ranch. I do."

Russ's fingers smoothed his short gray beard. "I see."

It was clear he didn't. "I didn't know until a couple of days ago, but it seems my parents bought the place and left it to me. My grandparents have been taking care of it. I've seen the deed, Russ. It's true."

"So why sell out? It's your legacy."

"No. I need to get a little place in town where my grandparents don't need to worry about caring for twenty thousand acres. Don't need to worry about road closures and power outages and an old house falling down around their ears." She grimaced. "Sorry. That's not much of a selling point." Especially not in this enormous, well-kept mansion.

Russ's hand rested on her shoulder. "Have you prayed about this?"

Had she? Not really. The direction was pretty clear without praying. "It's time, Russ."

"I don't know…"

"Please. I'll list it with the realty if I have to, but I'd rather not."

Kade's father regarded her thoughtfully. "It's no secret I'd like to own the land. Paradise Creek offers a lot of hay fields that would be a great addition to Eaglecrest."

"That's great." Cheri tried to keep the relief out of her voice. "What do you think it's worth?"

"I hate to see you throwing away the gift you have from your parents. I remember how much you always loved the ranch."

She raised her chin. "Those days are gone. And I'm not throwing it away. I-I'm repurposing it. I can't take care of my grandparents adequately on the ranch. And, I can't buy them a house elsewhere without selling first."

A grunt from the doorway to the dining room caused her to whirl.

Grandpa glowered at her. "Didn't I tell you to stop interfering?"

"It's my ranch, and you're my grandparents."

"You ain't responsible for us."

How could he even think that for a moment? "Of course, I am. You don't have anyone else, and neither do I."

Her gaze lifted just a hair. Behind Grandpa stood Kade, his eyes skewering her. How much had he overheard?

SHE WAS BEAUTIFUL. Her face flushed, her lips parted, her soft sweater curved in at the waist where her hands rested. Her blue eyes sparked at Chester then flattened when they caught sight of Kade.

He nearly reeled from the change. Not only did Cheri want rid of him, she wanted rid of the ranch. He knew that, but he hadn't known it was her choice to make. He'd accepted her decision once before — he'd married Daniela, after all — but how could he let her go again? This time there would be no ties to Paradise Creek or Saddle Springs. She'd be gone for good.

Kade couldn't let that happen. He just couldn't. Part of him reminded himself he must be some kind of fool to seek out pain and keep coming back for more, but he mentally batted the thoughts away like they were nothing but annoying insects. He would pursue her, and he wouldn't let her go. Not again.

It wasn't only his decision to make, and she'd said she wouldn't have him if he were the last man standing. But she'd come out to the stable to apologize and he... how had he responded? He'd pushed her away. Of course, he had. The pain he'd thought gentled had reared up and kicked its flashing hooves in his teeth.

He'd reacted.

If only he could take back his angry words. Would she have uttered hers? He'd seen the devastation in her face then the schooling of her features. What if he'd crossed the stable instead, pulled her into his arms, and kissed her the way he longed to? What if he'd forgiven her? Would things be different today?

"Maybe we should go." Cheri looked down at her feet. "If someone can take us home. I hate to be a bother. I'll call Paul Scarborough on Monday about getting the ranch appraised."

Paul Scarborough? Dillon's father. *No way.*

Cheri's gaze lifted to his.

Had he said that out loud? Maybe he had.

Dad put his hand on Cheri's arm. "Don't be so hasty, young lady. I didn't say no. You know it will take time to sell a spread like that. It might be on the market months or even years."

Cheri grimaced.

"All I'm asking is that you pray about it for the next few weeks. If, on New Year's, you can tell me you have clear guidance from God to sell the place, we'll talk." Dad's gaze flicked to Kade then back to Cheri. "Meanwhile, Gloria and I will do the same. We'll pray. And if we have clear guidance to buy, I'll make you a fair offer."

"But you already made an offer to my grandfather."

"Circumstances have changed." Dad looked straight at Kade.

Had Mom told him about their conversation yesterday? She must have, although Dad was fairly intuitive on his own. He certainly hadn't argued Mom's plans to take the team down to Paradise Creek and fetch the Mackenzies for Thanksgiving dinner.

Cheri pursed her lips. "I guess I don't have much choice."

"It's a big decision, and one you shouldn't make in haste. Choose this course as an action, not a reaction."

She stiffened and looked up at his dad. "I'm not sure what you mean."

"I think you do. We'll talk again." He patted her arm. "Would you like a seat, Chester? The recliner over there is comfortable and not too deep."

"I reckon we'd like to go home. Edith's not feeling so well."

Dad nodded.

"I can take you," Kade heard himself saying. "Give me a few minutes to hook up the team. Hey, bucko, want to go for a ride in the sleigh?"

Jericho looked up from the sprawling toy ranch where he and Harmony played. "Yeah! Horses! He'p Daddy?"

"Sure can." Having his son along would remind him not to do anything rash. Dad's recommendation for Cheri was good for Kade, too. Pray a lot, and see where things stood in a month. He nodded at Cheri. "Give me ten, fifteen minutes, and I'll bring the sleigh around front."

He strode to the back door, tugged on his cowboy hat and a warm jacket, then headed for the stables. His thoughts tumbled over each other like a litter of puppies at play and just as difficult to corral. But he'd start with Dad's advice, and not even reach for the harness until he'd poured his jumbled thoughts at the feet of his Heavenly Father.

"Lord, I need wisdom," he breathed. "So much wisdom."

CHAPTER 8

L ast time Cheri had ridden in this sleigh with Kade, she'd been happy and carefree and tucked tight against his side. Today a two-year-old sat wedged between them. Last time there'd been no one in the backseat. Today her grandparents and daughter rode there.

The crisp, cold air was the same, though. So, too, were the pines bowed with the weight of the snow, the river churning below, the hushed stillness only accented by the sounds of the horses — the steady plodding, the shshsh of the runners, the jingle of the harnesses when Nip or Tuck tossed his head.

How often had they followed the old trail beside the river rather than the gravel road winding up the mountain past Paradise Creek? Summer or winter. Springtime or autumn. They'd ridden horseback all through this area, and here — right in this clearing on a bluff high above the river — they'd lain on their backs watching a meteor shower and dreaming of the future. Of the beautiful home they'd build right here on the edge of Eaglecrest land, but not far from the headquarters of Paradise Creek.

When would her grandparents have told her the ranch was all hers? Would she have done things differently if she'd known? The familiar guilt and sorrow swirled in her gut. Life would have been so much better if only she'd resisted Dillon. She'd been in love with Kade, so why had she even been slightly tempted by Dillon's bad-boy vibe? She'd known he hated Kade. It turned out that's why he'd always flirted with her, but she'd been too stupid to realize she was only a pawn. Instead, she'd been flattered.

Stupid, stupid Cheri.

She'd taken self-defense classes since then, but that didn't mean she wanted to face him again and test her skills. It wouldn't be hard for him to guess where she'd come and follow her. She had to sell. Move somewhere less predictable.

Kade turned the horses and sleigh around the last grove of trees with a light touch of the reins.

Paradise Creek Ranch lay spread out below them. As a teen, she'd envied the much larger, fancier Eaglecrest. She'd been thrilled at Kade's attention, but she'd fallen in love with the man, not what his family represented. Yet, after six and a half years of running, nothing looked more beautiful than Paradise Creek with its crisscrossing fences and the neat rows in the apple orchard, the old log house where she'd grown up, the stable with its runs and corrals, the pump house and machine shed and the long-empty chicken coop. It was home.

She could stop running. Dig in her heels. Face Dillon Scarborough, evict the memories and the guilt, and move forward.

Could she do that? Really?

"Easy, easy." Kade's control of Nip and Tuck as they trotted down the last slope spoke to Cheri, too. Her heart slowed along with the pair's nimble feet. He had always been rock steady, never letting passion get away on him even when she teased.

So much water under the bridge.

"Hup, hup, whooooooa." At Kade's command, the horses slowed and came to a stop beside the shiny black pickup truck. "Stand." He jumped off the sleigh and offered his hand to Grandpa in the back.

With a wince and a set chin, Grandpa accepted help.

Cheri turned and clambered off the sleigh, remembering the times she'd leaped into Kade's arms from the seat. He'd twirled her around and kissed her soundly before depositing her on the ground.

"He'p me, Miss Cheri!"

She pivoted just in time to catch the two-year-old as he launched at her. On the other side of the sleigh, Kade's eyes locked on hers as he lifted Harmony down. Her daughter clung to him the same as his son did to her. Kade's jaw tightened as he lowered the little girl then reached for Grandma.

Jericho squeezed tighter as Cheri tried to release him. "Tanku."

"You're welcome, little guy."

"Pet Nip?"

"Okay." Cheri walked to the horses' heads and reached to smooth Nip's forelock from his eyes. "They're good horses."

Jericho nodded enthusiastically. "Good." He stretched out of her arms and hugged the horse.

Was Nip leaning into the hug? Totally looked like it.

The snow crunched as her daughter stepped up beside her and held her hand out to Tuck. The large horse snuffled against her flat palm, and Harmony giggled. "That tickles."

A thump over by the house drew Cheri's attention to her grandparents making their slow way up the few steps to the porch. Her heart stilled. Had she been wrong, pushing them to accept Gloria's invitation? But if they couldn't even handle this kind of outing to visit a neighbor, how could they possibly manage the ranch? Yes, they'd leased out the hay fields a few years back and had only kept a few horses, but even the house had suffered from neglect since her last visit. Add in the iffy power and road conditions, and it was obvious she needed to sell. She didn't need to pray about it. Her grandparents had taken care of her when Mom and Dad died years ago. Now it was her turn to look after them. Her duty, even.

Jericho wiggled to get down, and Cheri turned from the horses to release him. He ran to Kade, who lifted a shiny red toolbox from beneath the seat in the sleigh.

"What are you doing?" Her words came out sharper than she intended.

His eyes flicked to hers then away. "I'm going to fix the bathroom tap."

"Did Grandpa ask you to?" Because Grandpa never asked for help. Didn't welcome it.

"No. I noticed it."

"Why?"

He lifted a shoulder. "Why not? It's something I can do."

"We don't need your help." Now, why had she said that? It was obvious they needed all the help they could get.

"It's okay, Cheri." His voice hardened. "I'm doing it for your grandparents, not for you. Call it a thank you for taking Jericho and me in the other night."

They hadn't been overly gracious about it, mind you. And Cheri wasn't treating him any better right now. If only her emotions and thoughts would level out so she could think rationally. "I'm sorry. Thank you."

He tipped his hat. "That's better. Come along, bucko." He reached for his son. "Leave the horses alone now."

"Okay." Jericho slipped his small hand inside Kade's large, strong one.

"Wait. You're just going to leave the horses right here?"

"Uh... yes? I told them to stand, and they've been trained to the command. I doubt I'll be more than an hour. I'd like to get back to Eaglecrest before dark."

Of course he would. What had she been thinking, even challenging him about his horses? He knew far more about them — about driving a sleigh — than she did. What little she'd absorbed had been pushed aside as sheer survival skills had taken precedence over the past few years.

She took Harmony's hand and followed Kade and Jericho toward the house, trying not to notice the perfect fit of his blue jeans, the clip of his boots, the way his dark hair barely brushed the shearling collar of his denim jacket. His cowboy hat angled as he glanced down at his son, and the look of adoration on Jericho's face as he gazed back nearly undid her.

She'd shut the door on this life. Not only shut it, but slammed and locked it. Added a few bolts, and thrown away the key. She'd done it to herself.

Oh, God, what have I done?

It wasn't the first time she'd uttered those words, and it likely wouldn't be the last.

"You don't have to do this."

Kade looked up as Chester leaned against the door-jamb in the small bathroom. "Just wanted to say thanks for putting us up the other night." He sorted through the rubber washers in his toolbox. Which was the closest in size?

"You already did. Chopped up half a cord of wood. Left us food." Chester jerked his chin at the dismantled tap. "I was gonna get to that."

"Hard to pull a pipe wrench when you've got broken

ribs." By the rust stain in the sink, the tap had needed repairs long before Chester's accident, but Kade wasn't here to judge. He was here to demonstrate Jesus to the older couple as he'd agreed to do before the blizzard had blown Cheri into Java Springs. Hearing her voice down the hallway didn't erase his word to the other guys in the Cowboy Santa project. His word to Pastor Roland at the church.

He selected a washer and pushed it into place on the tap stem, retightened the nut, and wiped the assembly with a bit of wire wool.

"You done this before."

"A time or two." Kade reinserted the tap stem and reached for his pliers. "I'll tighten up the hinges on the pump house door next. Anything else I can do before I head out?"

"Why?" The word blurted out of the old man. "Thinkin' to spark my granddaughter again? She got other plans."

Kade winced. "Nope, that's not why at all." Truth was, if he hadn't been forced into the Mackenzies' driveway the other evening, he'd still be putting off making contact, Cowboy Santa or not. It would've taken all the courage he could have mustered, even with God's help. But then God had made it twice as hard while removing any chance of procrastination. Not that Kade was good at putting things off. His father had trained his boys up right, to face trials head on and do what needed to be done without flinching. Kade would have made an exception for the Mackenzies, though. There were a few other names on his list. He'd have started with them and gotten to Paradise Creek in good time. Like the day before Christmas.

He reached under the sink, turned the water back on, then tested the tap. Good. The drip was gone. He tucked the container of washers back into the toolbox and laid his pliers and wire wool beside it before closing the lid. "Heard anything about when NorthWestern Energy will be restoring power?"

Chester shook his head. "Ain't gonna be until after River Road gets plowed out, I'm guessing."

"Okay, I'll top off your generator then."

"Don't got more diesel. Edith's going to fill the picnic cooler with fridge stuff and leave it out on the porch. Weather's just above freezing, mostly. We'll use the outhouse and get on by until Monday. Won't be the first time."

"I brought diesel. Jerry cans are under the sleigh seat."

"You don't hafta—"

"Now, Chester, what kind of a neighbor would I be if I could help out and didn't? You're not in as dire straits as the man in Jesus' story about the Good Samaritan, but the principle's the same. You've heard that one, I suspect?"

The old man nodded. "Yep. Heard the tale. But—"

"The guy who lay on the road, all beaten up, would've taken anyone's help, but the theoretically good guys pretended they didn't see the situation and walked on by.

The foreigner everyone hated stepped in and helped him out. You know why Jesus told that story?"

"No, but I'm guessing you're gonna tell me."

Kade chuckled. "Jesus told the people to love their neighbors as they loved themselves, and some wise guy asked who his neighbor was. This was Jesus' reply. He reminded them they couldn't be selective. That their neighbor was anyone who was in need." Guilt stabbed deep. "I have a regret."

The old man's eyebrows hiked.

"Okay, I have a *lot* of regrets, but one of them is that I didn't stay in touch with you and Edith when Cheri left. I was hurting so much I didn't think about how it all affected you. I was a lousy neighbor, and I'm sorry."

Chester blinked.

There might've been a loose tear. Kade couldn't be sure.

"Hard times."

"Yes, it was." It wasn't a whole lot better now, seeing her again. Seeing the child she'd made with Dillon Scarborough. Maybe there'd be closure when she left this time... because she would. He'd heard the request she'd made of Dad, to buy her out. Of course, he'd known she would inherit one day, but his mind spun that she owned Paradise Creek now.

"Daddy? I hungry." Jericho peered around Chester's hip.

"Of course, you are. I'll get you something in a few minutes. Hang tough, bucko."

"Edith can fix him a bite." Chester edged back from the doorway.

A shriek resounded from the other end of the house. Kade dropped the toolbox to the floor, dodged the old man, and bolted for the kitchen.

CHAPTER 9

G randma!" Cheri knelt beside her grandmother. "What happened?"

"Can't... breathe."

Cheri fumbled for Grandma's wrist. Not that she knew how to take a pulse, but she also couldn't find any reassuring flutter. Oh, wait. There it was. Faint. Was it too slow?

Kade dropped to his knees on the other side. "Edith. I'm calling 9-1-1."

Fear slammed into Cheri. "The phone line's still out."

"I stuck one of the satellite phones from the ranch office in my jacket pocket. We use them all the time out on the range. After Tuesday's mishap, I'll never leave the house without one again." He stood and jogged to the entry. A moment later, she heard his steady voice relaying information.

Grandpa lowered himself to the spot Kade had vacated and put his hands on either side of Grandma's face. "Edith. Help's coming. You'll be okay, you hear me?"

Grandma clutched at his wrist, but her hand fell away. Her eyelids fluttered.

"Stay with us, Grandma. Breathe in and out." Cheri could hear the panic in her own voice. It was a solid twenty minutes from town under the best conditions, and these weren't them. And how long would it take to drag the paramedics from their Thanksgiving dinners and into the ambulance? Could they even make it up the unplowed road?

She jerked to her feet. What could she do? Something practical. Maybe a blanket. Grandpa had put a log or two in the wood stove when they'd come in a few minutes ago, but it was still chilly. She headed to the hallway and veered around the children.

The children.

They stood with their arms wrapped around each other, both staring with wide eyes. "Come with me, you two. Let's go find a cozy blanket for Grandma, okay?"

"Sleep on floor?" asked Jericho.

"Um... yes." Cheri's voice caught. "She's very tired."

"She fell down," Harmony said. "And you screamed."

Yes. Yes, she had.

Kade, still talking into his mobile phone, brushed past her. "Chester, they're asking if you have nitro spray in the house."

"Shore. In the basket by her rocker there. I shoulda thought of that."

Cheri grabbed both children's hands and towed them

down the hallway. What would have happened if Kade weren't in the house? Kade, with his clear head and his satellite phone? Would she and Grandpa just have sat there and watched Grandma die? Or would they have loaded Grandma into Kade's black pickup and started off to town on the snow-covered roads?

She shuddered. She hated driving in snow. Hated everything about winter. Hated everything about the ranch. Maybe New Mexico would be her new home instead of Michigan or Maine. In the shelter of her grandparents' bedroom, Cheri dropped to her knees and pulled both children close. "We need to pray for Grandma, okay?"

Harmony nodded, staring wide, but Jericho squeezed his eyes shut. "Pray Jesus amen."

Tears pricked Cheri's eyes. Oh, the precious faith of a small child whose daddy was raising him to follow the Lord. "Dear Jesus, please be with Grandma and keep her safe. Please help the ambulance to come quickly. Please help us know what to do while we wait." She took a deep, shuddering breath and tried to corral her thoughts. Could she utter the words? She choked them out. "May Your will be done. In Jesus' name, amen."

"I think Grandma would like this blanket." Harmony dragged a crocheted afghan off the foot of the bed. "It's like a rainbow with all the pretty colors."

Cheri nodded. "That's a good choice. Let's take it to her." But then what? Should she keep the children out of the room? But what if Grandpa needed her help? But he had Kade, who was far more useful than Cheri. How could she ever have thought she could take care of them as they aged? She was incompetent. Useless, really. She couldn't even have called for help.

Wouldn't it have been worse if she hadn't been home, though? How would Grandpa have navigated the unplowed mountain road in his old truck? He would have. Cheri knew that. But it wouldn't have been safe. Was the ambulance safe? Surely they had all-wheel-drive, good tires, and an experienced driver. How long would it take to come? Had even five minutes passed yet?

Harmony tugged Cheri's hand. "Come, Mama."

She blinked. She had to pull it together. For everyone's sake.

THE TRUCK SLID a little on the icy road as he followed the ambulance toward Saddle Springs. Kade kept both hands on the wheel and eased off the accelerator until the tires caught again. The lower part of River Road had been plowed up past the fairgrounds as far as Saddle View, the subdivision where people lived who'd made their money elsewhere and now played at ranching on ten acres or less.

That wasn't real Montana ranching. The Delgado spread had grown to over eighty thousand acres with the purchase of Standing Rock. Kade's grandfather and father — and now he and his brothers — worked that land every day of the year, come rain, snow, or blistering sunshine. The idyllic days were few, but it was in his blood, and he wouldn't change his or Jericho's destiny for a thing.

For Cheri Mackenzie?

He tightened his hands on the steering wheel and did not glance at the woman hyperventilating in his passenger seat. How had this happened, anyway? Just a few days ago he'd been laughing with his friends and making plans for the upcoming Christmas season. Then Cheri had blown back into his life — fittingly enough, on a howling winter wind — and suddenly he was totally embroiled in her life.

Lord? What are You doing here?

One thing was sure. He'd done a whole lot more praying the past few days, at least if quick pleas for help counted. They must, right? They'd be part of that whole pray without ceasing thing from Thessalonians.

A few minutes later, he pulled to a stop in the Mustang County Hospital parking lot. Cheri reached for the door handle, but he rested his hand on her arm. "Cheri. Make a plan."

"I can't. Grandma—"

"Cheri."

She stilled, staring at his hand then looking up at him. "What?" Those eyes, wide with fright, glistened with tears.

He couldn't help himself. His fingers brushed her face, wiping a stray tear. "Let's pray together. Then the kids and I will come in with you for a few minutes. Then I'll take you to Lauren's."

"I don't know, Kade. I can't just stay with someone I don't really know anymore. Thanks, though."

"She isn't a stranger." Kade quirked a grin. "You knew her in high school. She's a good friend, she lives just five minutes from here, and she's got room. I already called her. It's perfect." Other than it would start up Lauren's matchmaking juices, which already worked overtime.

Cheri sucked in her lip and dropped her gaze. "Your girlfriend?"

He tilted her jaw and cupped her face until she peered at him again. "No. She's just a friend. There's been no one in my life since Daniela."

No one else he'd wanted. Not like he wanted to close those few inches right now and kiss Cheri's soft lips. With her grandmother fighting for her life. With their children in the backseat, no doubt with wide eyes and listening ears.

He eased back, trailed his fingers down her arm, and squeezed her fingers. He closed his eyes before he could change his mind then uttered a short prayer. "Come on. Let's go."

Kade followed Cheri into the emergency room with Harmony clinging to his hand and Jericho riding his hip. When Cheri disappeared behind the desk, he settled into a molded plastic chair and pulled out his phone. He opened an animal match app Jericho liked and turned the volume to almost nothing. Harmony bent over the game with Jericho, and Kade stretched out his legs, leaned back in the uncomfortable seat, and closed his eyes.

Another prayer went up for Edith. For Chester. But then his thoughts latched onto Cheri. The anger that had resurged Tuesday had faded. Yesterday, he'd come to the conclusion that God had brought her back into his life temporarily so he could finally truly move on. But, now, he didn't want to move on. He could picture a new future with her, with these two children and maybe a few more.

He was crazy. He shouldn't be having these thoughts. Any softness toward him was only a result of the rug being yanked out from under her with her grandmother's heart attack. She wanted to sell the ranch and leave Saddle Springs — and Kade — in the rearview mirror. Again. Besides, she hadn't told him why she'd abandoned him that long ago summer. He couldn't trust her, but he did. Was he so gullible? She'd broken his trust before. Smashed it into a million pieces like the lamp that had gone over in the living room with him and his brothers wrestling years back. Nothing salvageable had remained.

His love for Cheri wasn't salvageable either. There was nothing left but a few painful shards.

Kade shifted on the seat and squinted at the children with one half-open eye. Jericho leaned against Harmony, who held the phone angled toward him. They giggled quietly as Jericho matched the *moo* with the cow.

Every moment he spent in Cheri's presence, his son bonded to Harmony. It was going to be painful for them both when Cheri and her daughter left again.

Unless they stayed. Unless Cheri came clean on the past and accepted Kade's love. His heart squeezed. Could it happen? Or was Kade a greater fool than most men?

THE STARRY NIGHT was still and dark as Cheri waited for Kade outside the hospital. How had he walked back into her life as though they belonged together? Depending on him came so naturally, but had there really been a choice? He'd stepped up, taken control, and kept Grandma breathing until the paramedics had taken over. He'd taken Nip and Tuck out to the stable after the ambulance left and settled all five horses for the night. After driving her to town, he'd assumed care of Harmony and found beds for them all at Lauren Yanovich's house. Lauren, still single, was now a veterinarian with her own clinic.

Cheri was torn. Torn between her daughter and her grandmother. Her past and her future. Paradise Creek and... whatever was out there.

The black truck idled to a stop at the curb. Before she could reach for the handle, Kade jumped down and rounded the vehicle. He set his hands on her shoulders and looked at her. Really looked at her. "How's Edith?"

Cheri sucked in a breath. "They're transferring her to Missoula as soon as they can. There's no cardiologist here."

"She's stable?"

"They're giving her oxygen and an IV for meds. The beepers keep going off and a nurse rushes in."

Kade pulled her close. One hand stroked her hair while the other tightened around her waist. His breath warmed her ear.

It felt as natural as breathing to sink against his strong

chest and wrap her arms around him. To draw strength from his calm stability. He'd always been solid, a rock in her life. But she'd betrayed him. She loosened her grip and tried to push away, but he only shifted his arms and held her tighter. Okay. Another minute wouldn't hurt.

Wait. Had that gentle touch been his lips pressing against her hair? Her heart battled against the memories darting against it like arrows from the enemy. *Not tonight, Dillon.* She'd deal with him later. There was no getting around it. She'd need to. But not tonight. Tonight she needed strength, and God had sent Kade. Kade, the only man who'd ever held her heart.

She tipped her head back to look up at him. His eyes hid in the shadow of his cowboy hat, and she reached up to nudge it back. The intensity staring back at her triggered a tremor the length of her body, and the chilly night receded.

Slowly, his eyes never leaving hers, he lowered his head until his soft lips touched hers. "Cheri," he whispered, then kissed her slowly and thoroughly until her knees buckled beneath her.

Oh, yes, she kissed him back with all the longing that six and a half years had left unfulfilled.

She was home.

CHAPTER 10

K ade spun a chair around and straddled it as Abigail set a coffee on the wooden table in front of him. "Hey, guys." Traditional Christmas music provided a quiet backdrop.

James tilted his gaze to the next table over, where Jericho waited patiently as Harmony lined up a row of gel pens in rainbow order down the center of the table. "What's been going on up top of River Road? Do your brain cells need electricity to connect?"

Garret elbowed James. "None of our business."

"I beg to differ. I've known Kade since we needed stepladders to mount up."

Kade chuckled. He remembered that day. He and James hadn't been much older than Jericho. Three, maybe? And the old mare had stood so patiently for them. "Can we just say it's been an interesting week and leave it at that?"

James shook his head. "Don't think so. You two are back together?"

Were they? That kiss a week ago said yes, but Cheri's texts from the city had only dealt with how her grandmother was doing and inquiries about Harmony. He'd phoned her over and over and gone to voicemail every time.

Sully had pulled her car out of the ditch, and she'd driven it to Missoula. She'd found a place for her and Chester to stay near the hospital.

"Hard to know." Kade shrugged. "Maybe."

"Didn't you learn anything the first time?"

"Dude, you're the one who decided I should take her to Paradise Creek."

"It was the polite thing to do."

"Then the avalanche covered the road thirty feet deep at the hairpin, and I couldn't get the rest of the way to Eaglecrest that night. My mom had the bright idea to bring them up for Thanksgiving, since your family couldn't come." He jutted his chin toward James. "And in between, I figured you'd assigned them to me for Cowboy Santa, so I might as well get started."

"And now you're babysitting her kid?" At least James had lowered his voice.

"A hospital is no place for a child and, this way, Cheri doesn't need to worry about her. She's got enough on her plate with Edith and Chester."

Garret chuckled. "Sounds like you're taking this whole Cowboy Santa thing to the next level. The way next level."

Kade shrugged. "I couldn't just walk away." Truth? He hadn't wanted to. At first, being around her had stung like salt in a wound, but it had seemed to get better. For a time.

"The plan was to do a good turn or two and make sure the families had presents under the tree Christmas morning. It didn't include babysitting for a week."

"Leave it alone. I haven't forgotten the others on my list. Just been a bit busy. They didn't get the power restored or the road plowed out until Monday. Besides, there's still three weeks to go. How are *you* doing with yours?"

"Nothing, yet," James admitted, turning to Garret. "You?"

"I made a list of the kids. How come I got so many? Lena Yang has five and Noela Bergstrom has three. What do kids want for Christmas, anyway?"

"Good question." James dropped his elbows to the table. "I've got Carmen Haviland on my list. Her kid is, what, four? What does a girl that age want?"

Kade glanced over at Jericho and Harmony. Jericho scribbled with a neon pink gel pen while Harmony bent over her own paper with a blue one, biting her lip and drawing slowly. Hopefully not another *family* picture for his friends to wonder about. "Art supplies, judging by that one."

"Yeah, maybe." James chewed his lip and tapped the paper in front of him. "Is Trevor going to do his list?"

"Yeah. Not Sawyer, though. He's not into it." Kade's younger brother had given a distant rodeo as an excuse.

"Trev and I can cover his if need be, so don't worry about it."

"If you two handle Evelina, and Garret does Mr. Samson, I can manage Dorothy."

"Thanks for not giving me more kids." Garret slapped James's back.

"Works for me." Kade gulped half his coffee. "Anything else? I need to swing by Manahan's Grocery before heading back up the mountain. If all goes well, Edith will be released in the morning."

"She doing okay then?"

"They put three stents in her heart and kept her in cardiac ICU for a few days. She's breathing okay on her own now, from what Cheri said."

James shook his head. "I still don't believe—"

"Cut it out."

"Whatever." His buddy rolled his eyes. "You'll look back and remember I told you so."

Kade shrugged. "Maybe. Maybe not. Either way, I couldn't just ignore them all." He drained his coffee. "I'd be okay with you guys praying, though. I'll admit this has been really weird, and I'm not sure of... well, anything."

Garret socked his shoulder. "You got it."

THE BLACK TRUCK was parked beside the old log house, just where it had been all last week, only now River Road, the driveway, and the yard had been plowed. Sunshine sparkled off the heaps of snow that had slid off the roof, and a blue plastic sled stood jammed in a drift beside the steps next to the stack of chopped logs.

Cheri released a long breath as she turned off the car's ignition. She'd spent an entire week trying to forget Kade's lips on hers and his strong arms holding her close. Trying to block the knowledge that her daughter was spending every day bonding with Kade and his little boy. Trying to focus on nothing but Grandma and her fight for life.

But her grandmother was recuperating, and Kade was here. Of course, he was. He wouldn't withhold Harmony from her a minute longer than necessary. He probably regretted his offer by now. He'd leave Paradise Creek Ranch shortly with a sigh of relief and no backward glance.

The creak of a door reminded her that Grandpa was already helping Grandma out of the car.

"I'll do that. Hold tight."

Grandpa glowered at her. "I'm fine." His ribs seemed to be healing, if his movements and facial expressions were any indication. That was good, at least.

Cheri exited the car and popped open the trunk to retrieve the bags she'd packed in haste a week ago while Kade stabled Nip and Tuck.

A shadow fell as Kade stretched past her. "I've got them." He set the bags down on the ice-dotted gravel and turned to her. His eyes searched hers with no hint of what he was thinking. "Welcome home."

"Thanks for holding things down." What would she have done without him? What she'd done for six and a half years. Fended for herself as best she could... but that hadn't included a ranch and horses.

He reached for her hands, but she grabbed the bags' handles. "I need to get inside and see to Grandma. Fix some lunch."

"Ruthie sent down a pot of soup and a pan of sourdough biscuits."

"Thanks." Why did he have to be so nice? So thoughtful?

"Cheri."

She focused on the top snap of his plaid flannel shirt where his jacket hung open. A brown shirt today. Matched his eyes.

His hand cradled her cheek, and she trembled but stood her ground. "I thought we'd maybe taken a step before you left for Missoula."

Cheri sucked in her lip. "A moment of weakness?" Feeble, like her voice sounded now.

"Not for me, and I don't think for you, either."

"Kade, this is a bad idea. A really bad idea."

His fingers trailed down her jaw, leaving every cell screaming for more. With all the inner strength she could muster, she managed not to lean into the touch.

"We've lost so much time, but the chemistry is still here. I believe God brought us back together. I've been praying. A lot."

While Cheri had been trying to shove it all into the recesses of her mind and not quite managing. Okay, not succeeding at all.

"Can I take you out tomorrow? Dinner at the

Branding Iron? And there's a new western playing at the theater."

How many times had he teased her about her thing for cowboy movies? Her heart yearned for life the way it'd been. Yearned to let go of everything that stood between them and welcome him back in. But that meant exposing the darkness. Meant confessions and vulnerability. Meant seeing the hurt and rejection in Kade's eyes. How could it not?

And, yet, he knew enough it should already be there. She'd left him before she found out she was pregnant. The devastating, overpowering guilt had been enough. She'd taken Kade's pure, sweet love and stomped it in the dirt.

"I-I don't think so. Things are rocky with Grandma still, and they really can't watch Harmony. I'd need a babysitter and—"

"She's pretty comfortable with my parents after this week. I can take her up to Eaglecrest. Jer would be thrilled."

"Kade, I don't know."

This time both his hands held her face, tipping it up until her only choices were to meet his gaze or close her eyes. Last time she'd done that in his presence, he'd kissed her senseless. Slowly she focused on his eyes. So brown. So clear.

"I think we need to talk. I don't want to lose you again, Cheri."

"Daniela..."

"Has been gone more than two years."

"But she..."

"Not really."

What did he mean? Cheri searched his face, but he gave nothing away. "But she was your wife. You loved her. She gave you Jericho."

Kade's eyebrows flickered and his mouth tightened. "Yes, I loved her. But my heart has belonged to you since I was twelve."

"But..." How could he say those two divergent things in the same breath? "Then I feel sorry for her."

He let out a mirthless laugh. "She understood."

That didn't even make sense. If she accepted his invitation, would he explain? Did she want him to? Because the Kade she knew wouldn't marry a woman he didn't love with all his heart. Even when that woman rejected him at the last minute?

Cheri swallowed hard. "Not in Saddle Springs. I don't want people to talk." She didn't want to be seen any more than she had to, let alone with Kade.

"Then I'll cook for you. My parents can keep Jericho and Harmony over at the ranch house."

Maybe this was even worse, being in his home, just the two of them. "Are you... above the garage?" He'd finished a two-bedroom apartment for them to live in while they built the dream house above the river. She'd picked out the cabinetry and paint colors.

Something flickered across his face. "Yes."

He'd lived there with Daniela instead of Cheri. She expelled a long breath. Wasn't this talk inevitable? Better to clear the air now, before he kissed her again and got her hopes up too much.

"If Grandma seems okay tomorrow, we could come for a couple of hours, I guess. I can drive." That way she could escape if she needed to.

Relief shone in Kade's eyes. "Five thirty? But I can pick you up and drop you off. Someone will need to feed the horses."

She shook her head. "I can manage the horses."

"Okay. If you're sure." He bent and brushed his lips over hers then picked up the bags and turned toward the house.

Lips tingling, Cheri stood riveted to the snowy parking area watching him stride away. Slowly her fingers covered her mouth as though hugging the kiss close.

At the bottom of the porch steps, he glanced over, and a grin warmed his face.

She snatched her hand away, but it was too late. He'd seen and drawn his own conclusions.

Which weren't exactly wrong.

CHAPTER 11

T hat's enough make-work jobs." Kade glared at his older brother. "I'll clean out Bowen's stall then I'm headed back to the house."

"There's more to be done."

"Nothing critical. I'll get to the tack room tomorrow. Or Sawyer can do it."

His younger brother snickered. "Hot date tonight?"

Kade leveled a stare at Sawyer and hoped no pink crept up his cheeks. "A long overdue talk is all." And, yes, with any luck, some kisses. The alternative was Cheri walking away again. This time, it would be for good. He blocked the panic that bubbled up.

"Look, she's bad news." Trevor stabbed the pitchfork into a nearby bale. "She's after something."

"Like what? She's already asked Dad to buy the ranch. And just so everyone knows, I'm not going to live down there without Cheri. It's all yours if Dad buys it, Sawyer."

Trevor crossed his arms. "Too rundown for you?"

Kade rolled his eyes. "Just because you're rattling around in a mountain lodge way too big for a single guy doesn't mean I'm jealous. Maybe instead of poking at me, you should look around for a woman of your own."

Sawyer dropped to a bale and looked from one brother to the other. "Yeah, Trev. Time to settle down."

"Or *you* could."

"Don't look at me." The youngest Delgado held up both hands. "I've got more broncs to ride. More buckles to earn. There's no woman alive who wants to put up with a rodeo cowboy. Not for keeps, anyway."

Trevor stared at Sawyer. "Or you could quit before you kill yourself. Don't you have enough trophies by now? Seriously?"

Kade took a sideways step. With Trevor focused on Sawyer, maybe he could finish mucking out the stall and hit the shower before five-thirty. Time was ticking by.

Sawyer pulled a straw out of the bale and rolled it end over end, never flinching from his brother's glare. "Nope. Never enough."

"Look, Dad hasn't built up Eaglecrest just for me, you know." Trevor jutted his chin toward Kade. "He needs us all to man up and do our share."

"*You* man up." Sawyer surged to his feet. "You're the oldest, as you've never let us forget. Isn't it your duty to get married and produce a son or two? As it stands now, Jericho is the only next-generation heir, and he doesn't even have Delgado blood running through his veins. Don't talk to me about responsibility."

So much for getting away from his brothers. Kade spun back. "Don't you toss that information around."

Sawyer shrugged. "Still true, and we all know it. He's cute and all that, but you sure complicated your life when you took on Daniela."

"My life was already complicated."

"Nothing compared to what it became, but then you knew that going in, right? Kade Delgado to the rescue."

Kade shoved his chest up against his brother's. "Don't mock me."

One of Trevor's hands clamped on Kade's shoulder and the other on Sawyer's. "Cut it out, you two."

Sawyer stepped back, hands in the air. "You know I like the kid. I've got no problem with him. Just don't talk to me about shirking responsibility around here when Kade can't do this and can't do that because he's got a kid in tow."

"I do my share, which is more than you do." Kade stabbed darts at Sawyer with his eyes. "And Dad and Mom knew the whole situation before I married Daniela. They agreed. Supported us both."

"The tack room—"

Sawyer spun to Trevor. "Shut up. We know what to do, and I'll do my share as long as I'm here, okay? Just so you know, I'm out of here Wednesday. Got a rodeo down Vegas way. Might be back for Christmas, and I might not."

"How is that not shirking your responsibility?"

"We've got plenty of ranch hands, and I'll be back for

calving, if you can promise to keep your high-and-mighty opinions to yourself."

"I'll have you know..."

Kade blocked his brothers and edged away. After all that, he barely had time for a lick and a promise for Bowen's stall. He grabbed the rake off its hook on the way by. Sawyer's jabs had struck home. At some point, he'd need to 'fess up to Cheri about the circumstances of Jericho's birth... but hopefully not tonight.

CHERI PULLED into the tidy yard at Eaglecrest, unsure whether to park by the ranch house or over by the four-car garage capped with Kade's apartment. The original attached garage had long since been taken over with the ranch offices then a second-story addition for staff housing.

She couldn't believe she'd accepted Kade's offer for his mom to watch Harmony along with Jericho this evening. She was so not ready to have this talk. To spend more than five minutes alone with the man she'd once loved. Gloria had been so welcoming at Thanksgiving and gone the extra mile — seven literal miles in a horse-drawn sleigh — to ensure Cheri and her grandparents had a good meal in a warm house. Then spent a week helping Kade watch Harmony, so it wasn't much of a stretch to think she'd be okay with one more evening.

Decision made, Cheri pulled up in front of the

imposing ranch house and shut off the ignition. "Ready?" she asked brightly.

Harmony's seatbelt unclicked. "Mrs. Gloria is really nice, and Jericho has lots of toys."

Of course he did. There was no shortage of cold, hard cash around here, unlike at the Mackenzies. Add to that, Kade's son had lived in the same place all his life. How many times had Cheri been forced to leave half of Harmony's meager possessions behind?

She held Harmony's hand as they took the three steps up to the partially-enclosed deck. Pine wreaths hung from the pillars clad with native Montana fieldstone on either side of the imposing entry door. Taking a deep breath, she reached for the bell just as the door swung open in front of her.

Jericho peeked out from behind his grandmother's jeans-clad legs. "Ha'mony!"

"Come on in!" Gloria smiled a welcome. "Kade just got in from the barn, and he'll let me know when he's ready for you to go on up to his place."

"Um, okay." This wasn't how it was supposed to go at all. She didn't exactly want one-on-one time with Kade's mother. The kids didn't count as a buffer. Harmony was already unzipping her jacket while Jericho spun in dizzying circles behind Gloria. They'd be off in a flash to the toy horses in the great room.

Cheri removed her boots, keeping her jacket on, then followed Gloria through the foyer, past the curving staircase across from the formal dining room where they'd assembled for Thanksgiving, and into the spacious kitchen at the back. "Thanks for watching Harmony this past week. I don't know what I would have done without your generosity."

Gloria waved a hand. "Not a problem. She and Jericho play so well together, and Ruthie and Elnora helped out."

"I appreciate it." Deep breath. "Tonight, too."

"I'm sure you and Kade have things to talk about."

Understatement. "I don't know..."

"Cheri? Keep praying, and see where things go. Don't write off my boy too quickly."

"I'm not sure how you can say that." She perched on a tall stool at the island where she could still see the view of the river tumbling between majestic mountains through the expansive morning room windows.

Through the archway in the great room, Jericho offered a horse to Harmony as he squatted by the miniature barn near the elegant Christmas tree. No wonder her daughter liked it at Eaglecrest.

"My son has been through a lot. He has a very sensitive spirit."

"He told me about his wife's death."

Sorrow lurked in Gloria's eyes. "She'd been sick for so long."

Cheri tilted her head to one side. "I thought she passed away in childbirth." Sounded like there was more to the story, but wasn't there always?

Gloria tightened her lips. "That will be his tale to tell. Can I pour you a cup of tea?"

Would Kade really be so long that this was needed?

Why hadn't he canceled, or at least called to let her know he'd be late? Phone lines up River Road had been restored days ago along with power. Thankfully, that meant Paradise Creek's dial-up Internet was up and running again, too... such as it was.

A buzz sounded, and Gloria glanced at her phone. "On the other hand, Kade must have taken the fastest shower of his life. He's ready for you. I guess you know the way."

Cheri exhaled. "Yes, I remember. Thank you." She looked through to the children's play area. "Harmony, I'll see you in a couple of hours. Be good for Mrs. Gloria, okay?"

Her daughter barely spared her a glance as the toy horse in her hand pranced around the room. "Yes, Mama."

She met Gloria's encouraging, knowing smile, and headed for the door. The short December day meant the sun had already passed the horizon, leaving dusk in its wake as Cheri crossed the yard. She hesitated at the door on the left of the four-bay garage. Through the glass, she could see the oak staircase heading up. Kade beckoned from the top.

Lord? I could use a lot of help here. Please.

Cheri opened the door, hung her coat on one of the hooks just inside then removed her boots and set them beside Kade's well-worn cowboy boots before padding up the wooden steps in her sock feet. The stairway came up alongside the living room and directly into the dining nook, where the aroma of savory chicken permeated the air. She'd painted this apartment a mid-range gray a few weeks before the scheduled wedding so the walls would be a great backdrop for the colorful artwork she'd planned. Someone had repainted it a golden yellow. Daniela, probably.

Stepping into this space ripped Cheri's heart in two. How could she have thrown away this man like last week's trash? How could he invite her back? Was he only doing it so he could be the one to shatter her heart this time? She lifted her gaze to meet his.

Kade stood across the island in the small kitchen, watching her with an unreadable expression. Yes, there should be a barrier between them. Physical, like the eating bar. Emotional, like his schooled features. "You came."

Had he expected her not to? He'd been right to wonder. She'd changed her mind about the wisdom of coming as often as she'd changed her clothes this afternoon, leaving a stack of discarded outfits draped over her bed in the old log house.

She nodded and crossed her arms over her chest. "Smells good."

"My slow cooker is my best friend." He thumbed over his shoulder to the counter by the stove. "I loaded it up this morning. I hope you like it."

Before, Kade had lived in the ranch house with his parents and brothers. A loft and three expansive suites, one for each son, comprised the second story. If Cheri had done any assuming, it would have been that he'd at least take his meals with his parents, since Jericho probably spent most daytimes there. She might even have thought he'd taken up residence again after his wife's death.

Instead, his kitchen looked lived-in but tidy. A wooden booster anchored one side of the small table, and a couple of scribbled drawings clung to the stainless, finger-print-free fridge with horse-head magnets. A Christmas tree with white lights and blue globes stood in front of the living room window. A shelving unit full of Jericho's books and toys lined the adjacent wall. On top of it stood a framed wedding photo, too distant to make out the details.

She swallowed hard. This was truly a home. A home filled with love and laughter before it had been struck by death. How long had Kade and Daniela been married before Jericho's birth? She'd been sick, Gloria said. So many questions needed answers. And Kade had his share of questions, for sure.

A moment later Kade had set two bowls of salad on the table and pulled aside a chair for her. Then he took a seat around the corner and held out his palm.

Cheri stared at it for a long moment before placing her hand in his.

"Father God, thank You for bringing Cheri here this evening. I pray that You would bless this food and guide our conversation." His fingers clenched slightly. "I ask that Your will be done in Jesus' name. Amen."

"Amen," she whispered.

CHAPTER 12

The fridge hummed, and the heirloom clock on the living room shelf ticked loudly. Every movement of a fork or knife clattered against the stoneware dishes. He should've put Christmas music on, should've known there'd be awkward silence. Now that Cheri was here, he had no idea what to say. It seemed she didn't, either.

She laid her silverware across the plate and dabbed her mouth with the linen napkin before setting it down. Half her food remained. "Thank you. That was delicious, but I don't have much of an appetite."

Kade's own plate hadn't fared much better. He pushed it away and rose to his feet. He and Jericho would be eating leftovers for days, which wasn't necessarily a bad thing. "You still drink decaf in the evening? I'll pour us each a cup."

"Let me help you clean up."

He shook his head. "Don't worry about it. I'll get it later." He pointed into the living room. "Have a seat."

While he cleared the plates, Cheri wandered into the adjoining space. She looked amazing in slim jeans with a pink-patterned top belted in at the waist. Her dusky blond hair hung in loose curls past her shoulder blades. Too late, he realized her destination. His and Daniela's wedding picture. He'd debated putting it away, but it'd seemed cowardly. Daniela was woven into the fabric of his life. He couldn't pull out her thread without unraveling everything, including Jericho. His grandmother had once cross-stitched a poem about life being a weaving with the dark threads being as needful as the gold and silver ones. When she'd passed on, shortly after Daniela, he'd claimed the framed poem as a reminder.

Cheri picked up the wedding photo and examined it.

Kade froze in the middle of his kitchen, a water glass in each hand, watching. What was she thinking? Could she see the pallor on Daniela's face?

"Tell me about your wife."

He inhaled sharply. He didn't want to talk about Daniela but, sooner or later, he'd have to, if he and Cheri continued forward... which was totally up in the air, kisses aside. "You first. I need to know what happened with Dillon."

Cheri set down the silver filigree frame and turned to face him, hands clasped behind her back. "I was an idiot."

She could say that again. He masked his expression

and kept his gaze fixed on hers as he set the glasses down beside the sink.

"He wouldn't let up flirting with me. Kept making innuendos and suggestions. Offering to teach me a thing or two." Cheri looked down. Her fuzzy gray sock polished the walnut floor. "He figured I'd been teasing him."

Kade remembered Cheri's power. Dillon wasn't the only one she'd enchanted without even trying. Or at least, she'd seemed blissfully unaware. In hindsight, Kade hadn't been so sure. His fists balled at his sides, and red clouded his vision. "Did he force you?" If he got his hands on Dillon Scarborough he'd punch the guy clear into Idaho. Maybe across into Washington.

Cheri stayed focused on her fuzzy sock. "Not... exactly."

Had he heard her correctly? She'd gone with Dillon willingly? How could she have?

She flashed a glance at him then turned away, cradling her arms around her body.

"Care to explain?" His voice came out harsher than planned, but maybe that was no surprise. The jerk had leered at Cheri for a year or two while making jabs at the Delgado fortune. Kade had once overheard a suggestive comment and given him a warning, but he'd never dreamed that Dillon's obsession ran so deep. The lout had bided his time, determined to ruin the beautiful thing Kade and Cheri had.

He'd succeeded.

"I can't explain. In my head, right then, it made

sense. I'd come to our wedding night with some experience. How could that be a bad thing?"

Kade stared at the back of her head. Steeled himself against her trembling shoulders. What had he expected to hear? That it had all been Dillon's fault? All the guys had been jealous of Kade. They thought Cheri was the bomb. They'd fallen all over themselves to banter with her and be rewarded by one of her teasing grins.

But Kade had been secure in the knowledge she'd loved him, only him. Until he'd driven into the Paradise Creek yard to pick her up for a trip to the florist in Saddle Springs to finalize the wedding bouquets. She hadn't come out to meet him. Edith had, while Chester stood in the doorway holding a shotgun. Cheri had disappeared in the night, leaving a short note anchored with Kade's ring.

Cheri turned to face him, her chin lifted even as tears dribbled down her cheeks. "I was wrong. I could blame Dillon. I could blame the liquor he plied me with. But the honest truth is, I knew what I was doing. Knew it could ruin my life, but somehow let it happen, anyway." Her gaze met his for a brief moment. "I've never been more sorry in my life for anything I've done."

She looked so miserable standing there in the middle of his living room, belying the cheery Christmas tree behind her.

He clenched the edge of the island to keep from going to her. "You should have told me. I'd have gotten rid of him. We should've stood together."

She shook her head slightly. "I couldn't face you. As soon as we'd… you know… I realized what I'd done was unforgiveable. There was no way to spin it right. To pretend it hadn't happened."

He opened his mouth to protest, but what was there to say? She was right. He wouldn't have forgiven her. Even now, it would be difficult.

"He followed me to Missoula. I didn't know he was there until he pulled in behind me at a twenty-four-hour gas bar. Told me I could never run from him."

Kade had probably still been in bed, dreaming of her soft kisses. Oblivious.

"For two months it seemed I was never out of his sight for five minutes. He waited for me outside public restrooms. He crowed when I began puking, proving my pregnancy."

Kade had held Daniela over the porcelain throne. Wiped her brow with a cool, damp washcloth. Cradled her limp body afterward.

"When he knew he'd ruined me, he let up on the surveillance and began staying out all night, drinking with his buddies. I began to plot my getaway. One night, I escaped. I drove for two days and wound up in a women's shelter in Dallas, where I stayed until after Harmony was born." Cheri's tear-filled eyes met his for the first time in her litany. "I hated her, Kade. Every minute she was a baby, I hated her. All I ever saw in her face was him. All I ever heard in her cries was Dillon's mocking voice. She was absolute proof that I was worth nothing, just like he said."

She'd finally said his name.

"That's not true, Cheri. You know it's not true."

She stared right through him. "I painted a mural on the shelter fence. A nearby business saw it and hired me to create one for them. Several more followed, and I began to feel like I could do this. When Harmony was two, he found us again."

What could Kade say? Nothing. Now that the dam gates had opened, she needed to keep talking until she was finished.

"This time, I was ready. I'd been saving my earnings, literally in a bag under my mattress. I'd taken a few self-defense classes and studied how to disappear more completely. I donned a short red-haired wig and stuffed my hips and top to look more rounded. I cut Harmony's hair like a boy. We got away, moving every few months until we landed in Arcadia Valley just over a year ago. For some stupid reason, I felt secure. Relaxed my guard. Got a regular job at a church-run daycare with an attached greenhouse. The Christian people I worked with became friends and I began to attend church. Began to believe God wasn't finished with me after all. And then Dillon..." She tightened her lips.

Silence stretched between them like an elastic band until Kade couldn't stand it anymore. "He found you again."

She nodded. "As luck — or God — would have it, I was off when he came to the daycare. Harmony had a dentist appointment. When Alaina described the man who'd come looking for me, I quit on the spot. Went home, packed, and hit the road again. I didn't know where to go, but with Grandpa's accident, I decided to come home for just a few days. I'd stay low and head out again right after Thanksgiving."

"Where to?"

Cheri shrugged, her eyes glancing off his.

"I'm so sorry all this happened to you." Yes, he'd been the jilted one. He should probably nurse his pain a little longer, but how could he, when she was so miserable? When Dillon had broken her, but God had redeemed her? Who was Kade to hold a grudge?

He reached around her, tugging her hands to the front. They were cold, clammy, but he gripped them, his thumbs caressing hers. "Consider staying?" The words escaped without his permission, without his knowledge, even, until they hung between them.

"I wish I could." Her voice broke.

He pulled her closer, and she leaned against him as sobs racked her body. Tears soaked the front of his shirt. He pressed a kiss to her hair, his hands caressing her back. Surely she could feel the protection he offered. The love that had never gone away despite his best efforts.

CONSIDER STAYING.

Could she? Was it possible to simply stop running? Sure, if she wanted to face Dillon again, but she didn't. She wasn't afraid for herself... not much, anyway. She was afraid for Harmony. It wasn't that he wanted their daughter so much as that he'd know she was the one final tool to ruin Cheri's life forever. No, she'd go toe-to-toe with Dillon if she needed to, but she'd do her best to keep him far away from Harmony.

And that meant disappearing again. She'd sit tight and hope for the best until Kade's father bought Paradise Creek from her. She'd have the papers drawn and ready to go on New Year's Eve, the house packed. It would be harder to stay on the move with her elderly grandparents as well as a child, but she would do what she had to do to keep everyone safe.

Safe.

Like the feeling inside her right now, enclosed in Kade's strong arms. Oh, God, why couldn't this last? Why couldn't Kade be the fortress that surrounded and protected her? No human could. It was God's job, but was He up for it? She'd thought so, in Arcadia Valley, when she'd eased back into church, when she'd rediscovered God's deep love. She'd thought she could trust Him... until Dillon reappeared.

Kade's fingers caressed her jaw, coaxing her chin up.

She knew what that meant. She wanted his kiss, his lips on hers, more than a woman on the run should.

"Cheri. Look at me."

If only... She met his gaze, his unfathomably dark eyes inches from her own. "Kade. How I wish everything was different."

"We can't undo the past, sweetheart." His soft, warm lips branded her forehead.

He probably didn't want to. That would mean no Daniela for him. No Jericho. Kade's and Cheri's paths had diverged six and a half years ago — two small children were proof of it — but at least Kade's child had been born inside marriage. Had been wanted. Loved from before his birth.

Cheri put her hands on Kade's biceps and pushed back. She needed air, sudden and desperate, but the hard muscles in those arms didn't release her so quickly. They rippled slightly under her touch, and she remembered the hours he'd spent chopping wood, the work of riding and roping and branding and fencing. Honest, physical work that left a man strong and healthy.

And then Kade's mouth covered hers, his lips teasing hers until she stopped pushing and her hands slid up to fork through his short hair. He emitted a soft groan — or was that her? — and deepened the kiss, one hand tucked around her waist and the other tangled in the hair at her neck, cupping her head. Holding her close. Murmuring words of endearment between kisses.

A warm feeling, freedom and joy, flowed through her. Not only that he still cared, even after all she'd done and the years that separated them, but, in that moment, she felt the love and acceptance of Jesus, too. If Kade could look past the sin that separated them, how much more could her Savior, who'd given His very life to redeem her messes?

CHAPTER 13

Two weeks had flown by, and Cheri was starting to believe in love again. More specifically, Kade's love. He hadn't quite said the words yet, but it shone from his eyes and curved from his lips. He'd come down to Paradise Creek nearly every day for little visits between his work on the ranch. They'd ridden out on Blaze and Bowen, with Harmony and Jericho tucked in the saddles ahead of them, and dragged back an evergreen to decorate with her grandparents' vintage ornaments. They'd cooked dinner together and Kade had challenged Grandpa to checkers and lost soundly. Grandma spent less time napping and more time knitting in her rocker, part of the household once again as she slowly regained strength.

Cheri had avoided going down into Saddle Springs. Instead, she'd accepted Gloria's offer to 'pick up a few things' while she was at Manahan's Grocery anyway.

Grandpa had written Gloria a check. Who knew those were still a thing?

But today — this evening — she braved the trip for Kade's sake. For Jericho's sake.

She slipped into the darkened church, clutching Harmony's hand, just as Pastor Roland welcomed the congregation to the annual Sunday School Christmas program. She blinked against the dim light. Where was Kade? He'd come down early for Jericho's final practice.

She barely recognized him without his cowboy hat as he beckoned from a pew near the back. But that was his smile. Now if only no one else saw her, recognized her, verbally speculated on why she was back in town, with a child, at her ex-fiancé's side. But, if things were to progress with Kade, she'd have to come to terms with being seen in public, right?

"Please stand with us, and let's sing *Joy to the World*," invited Pastor Roland.

Cheri, pulling her daughter with her, slipped in beside Kade as he rose. His fingers tightened around hers, and he gave her a little grin before beginning to sing. His strong, unapologetic baritone took her back in time to bonfires by the little lake on the Flying Horseshoe with their friends, where guitars ruled and country tunes had been interspersed with gospel choruses. James Carmichael had been a talented musician, and so had Lauren. Had they kept it up? And Kade's brother Trevor — they'd sang duets in church.

Now she lifted her voice quietly with Kade's. She

might hit a false note or two, but the words and music pulled her. *Let earth receive her King. Let every heart prepare Him room, and heaven and nature sing.*

The congregation hushed after singing *O Little Town of Bethlehem*, waiting expectantly. Spotlights shone on a makeshift stable housing a manger toward the rear of the stage. From the back of the country church came the sound of jingle bells, and seven or eight toddlers scrambled down the center aisle, shaking them gleefully, Jericho in the middle of the pack.

Lauren Yanovich sorted them into a line on the stage. A little girl in a ruffled dress burst into tears, and Lauren sat on the edge of the platform and whispered to her until she calmed. Meanwhile, Jericho and another little boy jumped off, the bells in their hands jarring discordantly. An older woman hurried over and lifted the two back up.

Laughter rippled over the audience.

Kade palmed his forehead. "Oh, man," he whispered.

Cheri couldn't help grinning as Harmony climbed on her lap for a better view. Weren't the two-and-three-year-olds always the stars of any Christmas concert? Maybe Dillon wouldn't bother her here where everyone knew them both, where Kade stood guard. Maybe she could just settle back in at Paradise Creek, at Springs of Living Water Church, in the community. Maybe next year Harmony would be onstage with the older kids, playing an angel, or maybe even the part of Mary.

Next year.

Did she dare hope?

Music came through the sound system — *Jingle Bells* — as the little ones shook their bells and sang out a rendition Cheri hadn't heard before. Jericho bellowed as he waved his bells over his head.

Kade groaned and sank deeper in his seat.

Cheri only hoped a parent closer to the front was capturing the moment in video. The kid was too cute.

Lauren gathered the bells, but not until Jericho had done another dance routine all his own. Then the music for *Away in a Manger* began, and the toddlers watched each other for cues for the actions that came with it. The little girl who'd cried lisped out the words, but Jericho dashed over to the stable and peered into the manger.

"Where Jesus?" he called out.

Kade leaned forward on his elbows and cradled his head, not looking. "Who thought this was a good idea?"

"What's he doing?" whispered Harmony.

Giggles shook Cheri's body, and it was all she could do not to let them erupt.

Others in the building didn't hold back as Lauren beckoned Jericho over. Not that he obeyed. He lifted a handful of hay and peered closer. "No Jesus." By now all the other children had given up on the song's actions and were staring at Jericho. A little girl ran over to inspect the manger with him.

Finally the music came to an end, and Lauren managed to get her charges off the platform and back down the aisle to resounding applause.

"I have to go get him," mumbled Kade. "Do you think they'd notice if no one claimed him?"

Her snickers let loose as Kade edged past her. Other parents also made their way to the back as the next age group of children came forward. Four and five-year-olds were slightly more predictable but no less sweet. Cheri clung to Harmony as her daughter peered, trying to see the performance of her age-mates.

Yes. Next year. God had brought her this far. Surely He wouldn't ditch her and her daughter now.

KADE HAD BEEN afraid Cheri wouldn't show up at all. Then he was sure she'd slip out during closing prayer, but she was still beside him as the lights came up and the people around them stood and greeted each other.

"Well, I declare!" Lauren's buxom mother leaned over from the pew in front of them, her gaze raking Cheri then Harmony before settling on Kade. "And to think I discredited the rumor I heard. No, I said. No, the young Delgado boy is smarter than that. No way he'd take her back after what she did to him all those years ago."

Kade laced his fingers with Cheri's before she could draw completely away. "Gossip is a nasty thing, Mrs. Y. You're right not to believe everything you hear."

"And with a child, no less. No wonder Edith had a heart attack. You must have shocked her senseless."

Patience was slipping. No, actually, it was gone. Kade surged to his feet, towering over the older woman. "Edith and Chester have been part of Harmony's life all along." He leaned toward Mrs. Yanovich until she took a slight step back. "Isn't it wonderful how Jesus came to earth to save us from our sins? He pretty much told the Pharisees they could only cast the first stone if they were perfect and hadn't done anything wrong themselves. You might recall the story. They all remembered somewhere else they'd rather be. A pressing engagement, as it were. Probably like you have downstairs in the fellowship hall."

Mrs. Yanovich's eyes grew wider with every word he spoke, and her hand pressed over her ample chest. "Oh, my goodness. Now I see where that unruly child of yours came from. Some respect for your elders, if you please."

"I have all the respect in the world for those who show respect in return." He pivoted, knowing his shoulders were about two inches from her face. He could feel the warmth of her breath, hear her stuttering. "Ready to go, Cheri?"

Jericho stood on the seat Kade had vacated, holding out his arms. "I ready, Daddy. Jesus here now. See?"

The teens had acted out the nativity story, and Mary had produced a life-size doll from beneath her tunic and reverently laid it in the manger.

Kade lifted his son and set him on his hip. "Yes, bucko. Jesus is here. I see." But did Dora Yanovich see? Did the other residents of Saddle Springs see? Oh, he didn't care what they thought, but by the stricken look on Cheri's face, she *did* care. "There's treats downstairs. Want to take a few minutes?"

She shook her head a smidgen. "I'd rather not," she whispered. "This has been quite... enough."

He lowered his voice. "Not everyone is like Lauren's mom."

"I know." Cheri tugged Harmony's jacket around her shoulders. "You can stay if you like, but I want to get this one home to bed. Handy we each brought a vehicle."

Only because he'd had to get Jericho here an hour early for the final practice. "Cheri, I..."

"Don't. I should have known. You know what they say. You can never go home again."

Were those tears quivering on her eyelashes? Kade longed to reach over and wipe them away, to gather her in his arms and kiss her until she believed him. That he didn't do it was more for the reverence of the church building than to keep their relationship hidden from the curious eyes of townspeople as they left the sanctuary. They hadn't kissed in front of the children, either. Kade was waiting. Waiting until he knew for absolutely certain that Cheri would marry him when he asked her this time. Because he would. He'd never stopped loving her.

"Daddy, I hungry."

Kade chuckled. "You're always hungry, bucko." He held out his free hand to Harmony. "Want to come for a cookie or two?" Yeah, he knew he wasn't playing fair, bypassing Cheri.

Harmony leaned against her mother. "May I?" she whispered.

"No, honey. It's time to go. Say goodnight to Jericho and Mr. Kade. We'll see them again in a few days, I'm sure." Cheri's gaze didn't quite meet Kade's.

A few days? He felt a stirring of worry. Were the accusations of one thoughtless gossip enough to break the bubble of rapport they'd been building for the past two weeks? He wouldn't let it happen, but he'd promised Jericho cookies, and he was going to deliver. Maybe he'd snag a few extras and stop in at Paradise Creek on his way past. Enough for Harmony and Cheri as well as Edith and Chester. Yeah, that's what he'd do.

Instead of kissing Cheri, he touched her shoulder as he edged past, carrying his son. "I'll see you soon." And that was a promise.

A HALF-MOON PEERED from between the clouds, offering enough light that Cheri could see the puff of her breath as she all but dragged Harmony toward the car. Coming in so late, she'd had to park beyond the brightly lit parking lot. She regretted it now. Regretted a lot of things.

"I wanted a cookie, Mama."

"I know, honey. Maybe we can bake some tomorrow." Not like the fancy ones the church ladies had no doubt brought to the concert. Cheri hadn't wanted to ask Gloria for things like icing sugar and chocolate sprinkles and teensy silver balls. But she could make oatmeal raisin cookies, maybe. Something to make up for leaving so hastily.

Cheri was so busy reliving Mrs. Yanovich's ugly words that she didn't register the shadow stepping out from between the cars until someone grabbed her arm.

"Cheri Mackenzie. I thought I might find you here."

Blood froze in her veins at the sound of Dillon's voice. "Let go of me." She jerked to free herself, but his grip only tightened as her mind blanked. Why couldn't she remember a single thing she'd learned in that self-defense class?

"I don't think so. I've wanted to get a good look at my daughter for a long time. You've kept her from me, but I have parental rights, too." He reached for Harmony.

The little girl kicked his shin and ducked away. "That's a bad man, Mama."

"Run," Cheri urged. "Go to Mr. Kade."

"Oh, that's a good one. Like Kade Delgado would ever come to the rescue of a tramp like you."

"I'm not a tramp." Cheri didn't dare turn to see if Harmony had obeyed her or if she simply hung back, out of Dillon's reach. "And Kade l-loves me."

"Well, maybe you two deserve each other then. You have a lot in common. You know he wasn't married all that long before his kid was born, right?" Dillon leaned closer, his breath mingling with hers. "Like six months or so."

What? Dillon wouldn't say that if it weren't true, would he? Not when it was something Cheri could easily verify. "A preemie?" She hated that she even asked, her voice shaking as the words spurted out on a light breath.

"Yeah, 'cause eight pounds is the average size of a preemie? No, Cheri. The guy you thought was so perfect got his girlfriend pregnant and only married her after he found out. Not so squeaky clean after all, huh?"

Kade hadn't wanted to talk about Daniela. He'd redirected every question, and Cheri hadn't thought it mattered. After all, Jericho's mother was dead. She was no competition for Kade's love, for his future.

Just like he had done the math as to when she'd gotten pregnant with Harmony, so she could count nine months, too. He'd told her Jericho's birthday was in September. The wedding photo in Kade's living room had been taken outside with crocuses at their feet. Eighteen months, maybe. Or six?

Why would Dillon lie? On the other hand, why would Dillon tell the truth?

"Kade wouldn't..." She zipped her mouth.

Dillon released her and laughed. "He wouldn't, huh? You're wrong."

"Why did you follow me here, Dillon? What do you want?"

"What's mine."

A hundred thoughts — no, a thousand — dashed through her mind like a herd of stampeding cattle. How could she get rid of Dillon once for all? She needed space. Space to think about what he'd said about Kade. She stared at him, trying to read his expression.

"Look, that was a long time ago." He held both hands up. "I'm not really as horrible as you think I am. She's my kid, and I want to know her. Contrary to what you seem to believe, fathers have rights, too. You're in contempt of court keeping her from me."

He couldn't be right. "There was no court." She hated the question in her voice.

"Just because you weren't there, doesn't mean it didn't happen." He leaned closer. "I stopped in to see Judge Kriegler on Friday. Your gig is up, Cheri. You run again, and when I find you, Harmony is all mine, and you're in jail."

CHAPTER 14

S o you guys are getting back together?" Lauren Yanovich smirked. "No wonder you said no every time I tried to set you up with somebody. I can't believe you carried a thing for her all these years..." Her eyebrows rose.

Kade tugged at his shirt collar. Lauren didn't have to say the words. No doubt they were, or would be, on everyone's tongues after tonight. Everyone in town would soon question his love for Daniela. But were the reasons for his brief marriage really anyone else's business? Not at all. Jericho perched on Kade's hip and chomped the head off a gingerbread man. Kade loved this kid like crazy, no matter his lineage.

Lauren's elbow poked his side. "Well, good for you. I was going to suggest Carmen Haviland to you, but maybe not." Lauren meant well — the polar opposite of her mother — but just as meddlesome.

"I've told you not to bother trying to set me up with

anyone." He eyed the woman in front of him. "Skip the other guys, too. We've got minds of our own, you know."

She fluttered a ringless hand. "But you cowhands are so busy and don't come into town nearly often enough to even know who's available."

Kade leaned closer, raising his eyebrows. "As a veterinarian, you do know nearly everyone in the county. Why don't you find someone for yourself?" The words, "like James Carmichael," nearly added themselves, but he bit them back in time. He didn't like Lauren meddling in his life, so why would she appreciate the other way around? To say nothing of James swearing him to silence.

"Oh, there's plenty of time," Lauren said airily.

Right, she was pushing thirty along with the rest of their classmates. Didn't most women want to have kids before they got a whole lot older?

He opened his mouth to take his argument a little further when he felt an urgent tug on his belt.

"Mr. Kade, Mr. Kade, come quick," Harmony begged. "There's a bad man got Mama."

Dillon? No way. Kade blinked then shoved Jericho at Lauren. "Here, you take him. Her, too." He pushed Harmony to Lauren's side. "Keep them safe." And he dodged through the crowd toward the exit, all but mowing Mrs. Yanovich right over.

It took a couple of seconds for his eyes to adjust to the bright rings from the parking lot lights... and to the darkness beyond them. Where was Cheri? How quickly had Harmony found him? He breathed a prayer that he wasn't too late.

A jagged laugh came from near the street. Kade tore down the steps and between the rows of parked vehicles toward the sound. In the light of a passing car he saw someone — Dillon? — lean over Cheri.

"No. It won't happen." But she didn't sound confident.

KADE DASHED UP BEHIND HER. Her elbow jabbed his ribs as she whirled, ready to take on any challenge. Even in the darkness her eyes flashed.

"It's me," he gasped. "Kade. What's going on?"

"No need to panic. I was just leaving." Dillon pinned Cheri with a knowing look. "I'll see you in a couple of days. No running, now. You hear?" He turned away, striding into the darkness.

"Are you okay?" Kade wrapped both arms around Cheri, but she didn't lean into him. "What was that all about? Is he threatening you?"

She shuddered and pushed away. "He says he has a court order to see Harmony. That he has rights."

Kade took a deep breath. He should've seen this coming. Would he let a woman take *his* child and disappear? Not a chance. "We can find out. We'll figure it out. Together." Why wouldn't she let him hold her?

"But I don't want him anywhere near her. She doesn't need him." Her voice shook. "Where's Harmony?"

"Inside. Lauren has both kids."

Cheri pushed away. "I need to see her. Make sure."

"They're safe. Everyone's safe." Kade reached out again, but she stepped aside, and his hands fell to his sides.

She gathered her hair into both hands and tossed it back, her gaze bouncing off his before she pivoted and strode toward the church.

He stared after her. She was *not* okay, no matter what she said. Hadn't they got past this point, to where she trusted him again to hold her and comfort her? Take care of her? But now the old Cheri was back. Independent. Evasive. Fearful.

And it drove Kade crazy. Daniela had needed safety and protection. Jericho certainly did. Even Kade's work with Cowboy Santa, which he needed to wrap up in the next few days, was a direct result of his driving need to fix things any time he could.

He didn't care about acquiring Paradise Creek Ranch. The Delgados had plenty of land of their own, to say nothing of the state lands leased for rangeland. All he cared about was Cheri.

So he could fix things for her? No. He *loved* her. Fixing was only part of it. Wouldn't any man want to shelter the woman he loved?

She mounted the church steps at the other end of the parking lot before he took a step toward her. He could follow her inside and, what, make a scene? Or he could wait out here, with the icy wind slicing through his thin shirt.

He'd go for option number three, and let things settle down a little. He'd roped James and Garret into helping him off-load a truckload of split wood at Paradise Creek tomorrow afternoon. That would give him time to pray, reacting with thought, and be soon enough to get to the bottom of whatever was going on in Cheri's mind.

He hoped.

"How was the concert?" Grandma asked as Cheri hung Harmony's coat back at the log house.

The concert? Cheri could barely remember. "Uh, fine. Good."

Harmony crossed her arms. "I want to do that next time."

"We'll see." Too much to think about in one evening. The concert, Lauren's mother, Dillon... and then Kade standing there in the parking lot without even a jacket on, but not following her into the church.

Her daughter stomped her foot. "But I want—"

"Harmony. Go get your jammies on."

"I'm hungry."

Cheri hiked her eyebrows. "Didn't you have a snack at church?" She'd found Harmony and Jericho at a table in the church basement with Lauren, a plate dotted with cookie crumbs in front of them.

"But..."

She turned her daughter and gave her a nudge. "Go brush your teeth." And that reminded her Kade had fixed the faucet. He'd mended the corral and some hinges and repaired Grandpa's snowmobile when the parts came in.

Was he doing all that out of love for her or some other reason? Why was she even doubting him?

Because of Dillon's words. Not quite an accusation, but simple facts so easy to check that there'd be no point in lying. A spring wedding. A full-term baby early in fall. Her mind whirled with the implications that Kade hadn't kept himself pure until marriage, either.

Not implication, but fact. A fact he hadn't bothered to mention when they'd talked about her past. Why had she wasted so much time worrying about what he thought of her when he wasn't that much better? Sure, he probably hadn't been engaged to someone else at the time like she'd been, but still, a pregnancy was a pregnancy. Right?

"Cheri?"

She started, staring at her grandmother. "Sorry, I was woolgathering."

Grandma frowned. "What happened?"

"Dora Yanovich happened." Cheri took a deep breath, glancing toward the hallway and the sound of running water in the bathroom. "And Dillon Scarborough happened."

"Oh, no." Grandma swayed and reached to the wall to steady herself. "Come tell us what we can do."

Cheri helped her grandmother back to the rocker in the kitchen, where Grandpa's gentle snores filled the air.

"We could sell the ranch and go somewhere else." Cheri plunked down on a nearby chair. It was no less than she'd already begun putting in motion, but hadn't pursued over the past two blissful weeks. She'd begun to dream it wasn't necessary, that maybe she could have her happily-ever-after, but with tonight? No. The community wouldn't accept her, Kade had hidden a very important secret from her, and Dillon thought he should get to know his daughter. The thing he'd said about a court order was a lie. It had to be. She'd test that somewhere far from Saddle Springs, Montana.

Grandma pursed her lips and studied Cheri's face. "I thought you'd gotten that nonsense out of your head."

"It's not nonsense."

Grandma smacked the back of Grandpa's hand with a bundle of knitting needles.

He came awake with a start, surging half out of his rocker until the pain from his mending ribs caught up to him and he sank back, grimacing. "Wh-what?"

"Talk some sense into this girl."

He blinked, shifting his gaze back and forth between them. "What's going on?"

Cheri sighed and delivered the short version, leaving out the bits about Kade Delgado.

Her grandparents exchanged a glance when she mentioned Dillon's words.

"Been wonderin' about that," Grandpa muttered. "Not that he deserves it, mind you."

Cheri shook her head. "He's bluffing."

"I don't think so. Pretty sure it'd stand up in a court of law. He ain't a felon that I heard tell of."

The whirlpool swirled, sucking her down with it. Away from Kade, away from Jesus, away from everything she'd ever cared about. Even Harmony was outside her control. Not that Kade deserved anything.

Grandpa eyed her. "I thought you were all taken up by the Delgado boy. He'd help you with this adjustment."

Grandma nodded at Grandpa's words and looked back at Cheri.

"I-I'm not sure."

Grandma snorted. "You been kissin' him like you're sure."

A flush crept up Cheri's neck as she glanced toward the hallway once again. No sign of her daughter. "What do you know about his marriage to Daniela?"

Her grandparents exchanged a look. "We don't get down to town often, nor hold much by gossip," Grandpa said at last.

She narrowed her gaze. "What kind of gossip?"

"Quick weddin' and quicker baby. These days half the time there ain't no weddin' at all, and no one seems to care one way or other." Grandpa shrugged. "It ain't on me to judge."

"She was pregnant."

Grandma picked up her knitting. "Seems so. Like your grandfather says, times have sure changed since we were young."

What, no woman had ever made a mistake like she had back then and found herself pregnant and on the run? But Cheri knew it was, in fact, different now. People didn't relegate the likes of her to the red-light district anymore. Didn't look down on kids like Harmony who were born out of wedlock. Who even used that phrase these days?

Still, the thought of Kade letting passion overrule his

sensible nature and getting a woman pregnant before marriage was incomprehensible. Anyone but Kade, who'd made so sure to hold his relationship with Cheri to the highest possible standard. So high she'd known he could never forgive her for what happened with Dillon.

Kade-the-perfect was about as messed up as she was.

The big question was, how much did it matter? Did he owe Cheri an apology for deceiving her? Oh, he hadn't lied in so many words, but he'd omitted telling the truth about Jericho's conception. Not that he'd cheated on the person he'd been engaged to at the time like she had.

Ugh. Her thoughts were all jumbled. If only the two paths to selling the ranch didn't require contacting Kade's father... or Dillon's.

Chapter 15

P lay Ha'mony?"

The million dollar question. Kade settled Jericho on his hip as he knocked on the door. "We'll see, bucko." Had Cheri settled down after the confrontation with Dillon last night? She hadn't answered Kade's call or text this morning.

The door cracked open to reveal Cheri's puffy face. She'd been crying?

"Hey, sweetheart." Kade put his hand on the door to nudge it open.

"Don't sweetheart me." Her voice caught. "Just don't."

He blinked as Jericho's arms tightened around his neck. "Cheri, I—"

Her gaze flitted to his son then back to him. "How long were you married when he was born?"

Oh. His heart deflated as he grabbed for breath. "I can explain."

She let out a sardonic laugh. "I bet you can. She was pregnant, wasn't she?"

"Well, yes, but it's not what you th—"

Cheri leaned into the gap between the door and the jamb. "I'm not stupid, Kade Delgado. I know how babies are made. I took Mrs. Merino's sex ed class in seventh grade same as you did — plus, you know, I have a child."

"Cheri, please. Let me explain."

Jericho grabbed Kade's face between both mittened hands. "Daddy, play Ha'mony."

The grinding of gears on a big truck coming down the driveway became louder. His friends and the firewood would be around the final corner in a few seconds.

"Just admit it, Kade. It doesn't take a genius to figure out what happened. A bit too much snuggling, and..."

He tightened his jaw. "The story is longer than that, and there isn't time now. Would you come up to Eaglecrest later or tomorrow? Mom or Ruthie can watch the kids so we can go for a ride. Talk."

The dump truck rumbled into the yard.

Cheri's eyes narrowed. "What's that?"

"James and Garret and a load of firewood."

"Did my grandfather ask you to do this?"

Kade hesitated. "No, he didn't, but I know the situation around here and—"

"We can manage fine. We don't need charity, or that much wood since we aren't going to be living here through the winter."

He stared at her as his heart dropped. "What are you saying?"

"I'm getting us a rental until the ranch is sold." She didn't meet his eyes. "Sorry Jericho can't come in to play, but Harmony and I are driving into town right now to view a couple of places."

Kade lifted a hand to touch her face, but she pulled back through the narrow gap. "Cheri, don't cut me out."

"Yo, Delgado! Where do you want this load dumped?" hollered Garret.

Kade turned to reply as the door shut with a firm click. This couldn't be happening, but he couldn't deal with everything at once. Firewood first. Cheri second. He hadn't wanted to tell her Daniela's story yet, but he hadn't thought how it would look to her if he didn't.

Shooting a quick prayer heavenward, he strode across the yard and pointed to an open spot near the dwindling row of split logs.

Garret backed the truck closer then dumped the load. The logs tumbled out with a loud rumble, and Jericho clamped both hands over his ears.

What was Kade going to do with his toddler? He hadn't expected Cheri to refuse Jericho, but then he hadn't expected her to throw Daniela's pregnancy at him right now, either. The boy certainly wouldn't be safe with three men tossing and stacking logs. Best bet was to stick him in the cab, making sure the brake was firmly set. Kade lowered the windows a few inches and tucked his son inside. "You can watch Daddy from here, okay?"

"Play Ha'mony."

"Sorry, bucko. Not this time."

Jericho's face puckered and tears pooled in his eyes. "Play."

Kade gave his son a hug. "Don't cry. See Uncle James and Uncle Garret? See how quickly we can get the firewood put away. You watch, okay?"

Jericho let out a wail and slumped into the seat.

Great. Kade wasn't going to be much help with his son perched on his hip. Maybe they could just work quickly. Maybe Jericho would stop crying in a minute. He'd settled down to a few whimpers when Cheri dragged Harmony past the truck to her car a few minutes later then drove away. Jericho stood on the seat and watched the car disappear.

Kade knew how the boy felt. He worked as quickly as he could stacking the split logs his friends heaved his direction.

"What's going on?" James asked at last. "You looked all cozy at the concert. Now she's not talking to you?"

"Seems like." Kade clenched his jaw. "Dillon is in town."

"You're kidding me. She's back with him?"

Thoughts assaulted Kade. She wouldn't, would she? Just to keep the semblance of a family for Harmony? She wouldn't. "No, but it threw her for a loop." Which begged the question, where had Cheri heard about Daniela? Mrs. Y. hadn't tossed out that information. Had Dillon?

"What's going on here?" Chester's voice came from the porch. "I don't recall orderin' firewood."

"You didn't tell them?" asked Garret.

Kade winced. "I didn't have time. Be right back." He

strode over to the porch, but leaned against the railing with one foot on the bottom step so he wouldn't tower over the older man. "Hey, Chester. The guys are just delivering a load ordered by Springs of Living Water Church." Via Kade.

Chester's eyebrows drew together. "The church? We ain't members there."

"I know. We're just giving a helping hand to some families in the community who could use it."

"I don't hold much by charity."

Kade nodded. "I get it. No strings attached, though."

The old man shifted as he peered over at the other two guys, still stacking wood. "Never had much use for church or the hypocrites who go there."

"They're only people, same as anyone else. The only real difference is they've come to understand they need God's help and forgiveness, and they're trying to live with the Bible as their guidebook."

"Humph. Who do I make a check out to?"

"For the wood?"

Chester nodded.

"No one. It's a gift."

"But..."

"It's okay to accept it. Gifts aren't something we earn or pay for. Then they wouldn't be gifts."

The old man scratched his head. "I don't rightly know..."

"It's coming on Christmas, and that's the time we celebrate God's greatest gift for this planet, His son, Jesus."

"Don't start."

"God loves you, Chester. You and Edith both. He'd love to welcome you into His fold. You heard the Bible story of the lost lamb? This here—" Kade waved his hand "—is one of the ways God is showing His love to you through your neighbors."

"Humph. Well, thanks." Chester shuffled back a step and shut the door.

Kade grinned as he turned back to the work site and waved at Jericho staring out the truck window. Cowboy Santa was all about sowing seeds. Here was one well planted.

CHERI STARED AT LAUREN YANOVICH. "I didn't realize..."

Her former schoolmate jiggled a set of keys. "It's the other half of the duplex. Might be a bit small for the four of you, but it does have three bedrooms. One down, two up."

"I don't know." Today wasn't going as she'd planned but, then, neither had yesterday. She straightened her spine. It was only temporary. Just until the ranch sold, and they could go elsewhere. Either Russ would buy it, or she'd list it with Paul's real estate company.

She'd stopped by the courthouse, and the clerk had confirmed Dillon's words. Her days of running from him were over *or else*. But that didn't mean she wanted the ranch, wanted to stay anywhere near Kade Delgado any longer than it took to get well rid of everything.

"Here. I'll show you around." Lauren jogged down the steps and over to the matching ones a few feet away. "Carmen Haviland and her daughter lived here until recently, then she moved out to the Rocking H. Do you remember Carmen? She used to visit here a lot when we were all kids. Carmen Davis."

Carmen. Carmen Davis. "I'm not sure."

"She married Eric Haviland, but he was killed when a bull gored him in a rodeo."

"Oh, no. That sounds terrible."

Lauren opened the door to the other half of the building and ushered Cheri and Harmony inside. "That was three years ago. Eric was supposed to inherit the Rocking H, but old Howard cut Carmen out of the will in favor of his other great-nephew, who hasn't even visited in years. She's some ticked off with him. She loves that ranch."

"Umhmm." Cheri glanced around the duplex. The house at Paradise Creek was no mansion — especially not compared to Eaglecrest — but it was spacious compared to this place. "A main floor bedroom?"

Lauren pointed. "Right through there."

The small space would barely house her grandparents' queen-size bed, let alone their end tables and dresser. Small closet, too. Cheri pursed her lips. Galley kitchen with dining nook. Compact living room. Bathroom too small for a walker. She looked up the steep staircase. "Come on, Harmony. Let's see what's up there."

The answer was two small bedrooms and a tiny half bath. The front bedroom, slightly larger than the other, overlooked a busy street corner in the heart of Saddle Springs.

In her mind's eye, she could see her grandparents frowning and shaking their heads. They weren't going to be thrilled with these cramped quarters. Well, neither would she, but the other rental had already been snapped up, and there wasn't much else available. Looked like most people were smart enough not to be moving in the middle of a Montana winter if it wasn't necessary.

It *was* necessary. Cheri couldn't take care of her grandparents so far from town, not with Grandpa's ribs and Grandma's heart. They needed to be close to the hospital, close to a paved road that was kept plowed.

But this duplex? She cringed inwardly as she turned to Lauren, who'd followed her up. "Can I let you know on Wednesday?"

"Sure. I can hold it for forty-eight hours. I do have someone coming over tomorrow to have a look." Lauren held up both hands. "That's not meant to be a sales pitch. It's only a fact."

"Okay. Good to know." If only it were a little larger, Cheri wouldn't hesitate, but she really should mull it over a bit longer and consider the logistics. Try to talk her grandparents into the move as a reality not a theory. Yeah, it wasn't going to go over well.

"Good to see you and Kade getting back together. I'm surprised you're moving down to town, that much further from Eaglecrest."

"Um, I'm not sure we're together."

Lauren's eyebrows shot up. "Oh? What happened last

night, if you don't mind my asking? I'm sorry if it was my mom. She can be something else, for sure."

She *did* mind, but Lauren had been good enough to watch Harmony while Cheri duked it out with Dillon. "No, it wasn't your mom." At least, not completely. "I'm just not sure Kade's a good idea." Cheri eyed Lauren. The other woman seemed willing to talk about anything and anyone. She might be a good source of information. "What can you tell me about Daniela?"

Lauren pulled back. "Daniela? Kade's wife? She's been gone for over two years. She's no competition, if that's what you're worried about."

"I know she's dead. How long were they married?" She already knew the answer.

"A few months or so. I don't remember exactly."

"She was pregnant when they got married."

Lauren shrugged. "Guess so, but that shouldn't bother you. It's like the pot calling the kettle black."

"I can't believe you said that." Cheri chipped the words out.

"Sorry, but it's true. Everyone messes up one way or another. You and Kade have that in common, but he's a strong Christian, so don't worry about that."

It would be nice if Lauren stopped telling her what she should or shouldn't worry about.

"He's a great guy, and Jericho is such a sweetie. The little guy needs a mommy as much as your daughter needs a dad. Plus, you and Kade had such a good thing going." Lauren chuckled. "I've tried to convince him to date Carmen or Tori or one of the other singles in our church, but he keeps telling me to mind my own business."

A spark of jealousy flared in Cheri's chest. "Maybe you want him yourself?"

Lauren shook her head. "Are you kidding? I want a guy who loves only me, not the two women who left him high and dry."

Two women? Oh. Cheri and Daniela.

"Listen, *you* may not know if you're together, but I don't think Kade has any such doubts. You didn't see how he was looking at you last night. You didn't see the expression on his face and the speed with which he ran out of the church when Harmony called him. He loves you, Cheri. You'd be crazy to let him get away."

Lauren was right. All evidence pointed to Kade's devotion to her, even after everything that had happened. Even right now, he was up at Paradise Creek stacking firewood for her grandparents. For her.

Maybe she should hear him out about Daniela. But what could he possibly say that would wipe away the truth? He'd gotten his wife pregnant before marrying her.

But then, why was she holding him to a higher standard than she'd held herself?

CHAPTER 16

C *an we talk?*

Kade stared at the text on his phone. After two days of radio silence, *now* she wanted to talk? When he was about to leave Jericho with his parents and drive into town to meet the guys to deliver the Cowboy Santa boxes to the families on their lists? He'd planned to drop off the Mackenzies' box on the way home and hope he didn't have to leave it out on the porch.

Sure. I have to run some errands in SS. Want to come along?

If it were just for him, he could put it off, but not with Christmas Eve tomorrow and the guys waiting for him. But twenty minutes on the way to town would be enough to tell his story and let her digest it... or not. If not, it was going to be a rough afternoon on them both.

It couldn't be helped.

I guess so. I'll make sure it's okay with Grandma to watch Harmony.

Kade cringed. It had been less than a month since the heart attack, and it didn't seem right to leave Edith with the little girl. On the other hand, Harmony lived there and could be entertained for hours with some blank paper and a package of gel pens.

I'm leaving in ten minutes. See you then.

Okay.

She didn't sound overly enthusiastic, but he could sympathize. From where she stood, his story could only go one way.

"Come on, bucko." He reached for Jericho. "Time to go over to Grandma's. You can play with the toy horses."

His son looked up, frowning. "Ha'mony play?"

"Not this time." But, Lord willing, maybe soon.

TEN MINUTES HADN'T GIVEN Cheri long to change into her nicest jeans and soft blue top, brush her hair, and touch up her makeup. All that after settling Harmony at the kitchen table.

"You sure about this?" asked Grandma.

Cheri pushed out a confident smile. "Yep." The truth? She wasn't sure at all.

"You could do worse," mumbled Grandpa around the latest copy of Working Ranch.

Kade's diesel pickup rumbled into the yard. Cheri bent to kiss her daughter's forehead. "You be good for Grandma and Grandpa. I don't know what time I'll be back." She'd noticed he hadn't said what kind of errands or how long they'd take. And walking home if this talk went poorly wasn't an option.

She breathed a prayer as she settled her coat over her shoulders, tugged on her boots, and opened the door as Kade's hand lifted to knock. "Hi."

His dark eyes searched hers as a little smile tugged at his lips. "Hi yourself. You look great. Ready?"

She nodded but didn't take his hand as they crossed to his idling truck. He opened the door and she clambered in. A moment later they were headed up the long winding drive. In her periphery, she caught his glance several times, but what could she possibly lead off with?

"It's time to tell you about Daniela."

"I have something to say first."

Kade glanced at her. "Okay."

"Whatever happened with your wife isn't any of my business." Not that she wasn't curious. "God poked me, hard, about my attitude. I mean, I assume you knew what you were doing, but I was worse about Dillon. Or I could have told you instead of running. Trusted you. I did a terrible thing..."

Kade's jaw hardened as he turned the truck onto River Road. "Look, I'm not perfect, but—"

"I know. That's what I'm trying to say. God doesn't see it all that differently. It's just that—"

"Cheri."

She snuck a glance at him, taking in the silhouette of his chiseled jaw, his straight nose, the cowboy hat pulled low over his forehead. She tucked her hands under her thighs lest she reach across the cab and touch his face.

He whooshed out a long breath. "Please let me tell you about Daniela."

"Okay." Whatever he said, she wasn't going to let it bother her. Unless he was still so in love with his dead wife that he couldn't move forward. He wouldn't say that, though. He'd already proved history was where it belonged.

"I met Daniela through Lauren. You know she's always trying to match people up."

Cheri nodded. Lauren had even admitted as much, though not about Daniela and Kade.

"Daniela came to Saddle Springs after her boyfriend had been killed in an accident and she was trying to figure out her options. She wasn't well. It was a tough time for her, looking for a job, a place to live, and dealing with health issues. Working through things spiritually."

If Kade wanted Cheri's sympathy for Daniela's sob story, he needed to try harder.

"She found out two things at about the same time. One, that she had cervical cancer, and two, that she was pregnant." He looked across the cab as though trying to gauge Cheri's response.

"Aren't you leaving something out?"

His eyebrows drew together. "No?"

"Oh, come on, Kade. You guys were sleeping together!"

"What? No."

"Babies come from somewhere. Only Mary had an immaculate conception."

"Cheri. Didn't you hear me? I said her boyfriend died. He's the one who got her pregnant, not me."

Silence penetrated the truck for a long moment while Cheri struggled to breathe. Her mind rearranged all the pieces of information she'd acquired. She'd assembled them into one picture, but her assumption wasn't the only image they could make. "Jericho's not your son?"

"My name is on his birth certificate."

Her mind whirled. "But how? Why?" And here she'd even told him how much Jericho looked like him.

"The doctors wanted her to abort. They refused to treat the cancer if she was pregnant. Chemo and radiation would have killed the baby just as surely."

"She refused treatment?" What a decision to face. Would Cheri have made the same one? Her heart sank as she remembered discovering she was carrying Dillon's child. No question. She'd have chosen the abortion if there'd been any way to assuage her guilt over doing so.

"Yes. She refused." Kade's hands flexed on the steering wheel. "The cancer was already Stage Three when they found it. Even with treatment, her odds wouldn't have been very good."

"Why did you marry her?" Cheri whispered.

"A few reasons. I wasn't over you, Cheri. I didn't think I'd ever love again, but Daniela was okay with that so long as I could love her child like my own. That's never been a problem. He's mine in every way that counts."

"What else?"

"I could give her a home. I could take care of her,

both physically and medically. She needed someone, and I believe God called me to step into the gap for her."

"You're too good for me." Just like she'd assumed before hearing the whole story.

"No, Cheri. I'm a sinner saved by God's grace, same as you. Just because I didn't sleep with Daniela doesn't mean I haven't done other things. God doesn't measure or categorize sin."

She knew his words were true, but had a hard time really believing it. She always had. It wasn't like she'd told a little white lie or eaten someone else's sandwich from the fridge at work.

"It's Satan who tells us we're too terrible for God's grace. He uses every means possible to keep us in bondage, unable to enjoy living in the light." He glanced at her. "I'm sorry I didn't tell you sooner. Probably most people in town assume what you did, and I haven't bothered to set the record straight. To me, it doesn't matter. Jericho's my son."

"But you didn't love your wife." He'd loved her, Cheri, when he married Daniela. Did he still?

"No, I didn't. I came to love her, though. She had a sweet, giving nature. If she could have beat the cancer, I would still be contentedly married to her."

That put another spin on it. A glance out the truck window revealed the bridge and, beyond it, Saddle Springs. "Kade, I... I have to think about this."

He nodded. "I get it."

"What are you doing in town? Picking up groceries?"

"I can stop at Manahan's if you want to." He looked

ready to say more but shut his mouth as they trundled across the bridge. "Just meeting the guys over at the church to pick up and deliver some packages," he added at last.

"What kind of packages?"

"Christmas things for some of the elderly and a few single moms." He shot her a sidelong look.

A few more pieces clicked into place, pieces of a different puzzle. Cheri swiveled to face him more fully. "Packages like loads of firewood?"

Kade shifted in his seat and averted his gaze. "Those have already been delivered."

"So it wasn't because of me?"

"Your grandparents were on the list before you came home." He bit his lip. "I figured it was time to show God's love to my neighbors."

"So they'd like you more and sell you the ranch."

"No, Cheri. It wasn't that way at all. Not even close."

"What am I supposed to think?"

"You're the one who wants to sell the land. Not your grandfather."

"Because it was never his."

"You coming home didn't negate your grandparents' need for help. Chester's accident was followed closely by Edith's heart attack. Do you really begrudge the little help I've been able to give, just because Springs of Living Water Church foot the bill and not me? I've been the hands and feet, glad to do it for them. Glad to do it for you."

Was Kade really as perfect as he seemed? She'd

thought he had an Achilles' heel where Daniela was concerned, but now she wasn't so sure. But this, this was almost too much.

"I NEED to grab my boxes and get rolling." Kade lifted the one labeled Donovan and pivoted for the door.

"What's your hurry, man?" Garret laughed. "We've got all day."

"You might. I don't." Not with Cheri waiting.

Trevor chose that moment to stroll in. "Why is Cheri sitting out in the truck?"

"Waiting for me."

"She should've come in where it's warmer."

"She didn't want to." She'd been pensive since his confession, and he hated leaving her for long.

"She's talking to you again?" asked Garret.

Trevor swung to face him. "Did I miss something?"

Thanks, Garret. "Just a hiccup. No worries." If only Kade believed that himself, but there were reasons he rarely confided in his brother. Trevor might be older by only eighteen months, but he made sure no one forgot.

"Can't trust women," grumbled Trevor. "Don't go doing something stupid like proposing to her again."

"Not today," promised Kade. He wouldn't let the guys know he'd dug the ring Cheri had returned six and a half years ago out of the sock at the back of his drawer and prayed over it last night.

"At least you've got Lauren off your back." James

shook his head. "She's full of ideas for whom I should date."

Garret turned to James. "Really? She's only tried to set me up twice. How come you're so special?"

"Just ask her out already," advised Trevor.

"Who?" Garret looked between them. "What am I missing?"

Kade chomped the inside of his cheek to keep from grinning. "I'll be right back for a couple of more boxes." He headed for the steps.

"No, really, who?" he heard Garret ask behind him.

Kade set the box in the truck bed then opened the passenger door. "Just a few more to haul up." A few days ago, he'd have leaned in for a kiss while he was here, but the expression on Cheri's face forestalled him.

"I'm with Trevor," Garret said as Kade came back into the basement. "If you like her, ask her out already."

"Leave me alone, okay? She doesn't like me that way. We're just friends."

"*We're just friends*," Trevor mocked in a falsetto before returning to his regular voice. "People have gone from just friends to in love before, you know. Where are my boxes?"

"Does she try to set *you* up with women, too?" Garret asked Trevor. "I'm trying to decide if maybe she thinks I'm a bad pick for anyone, since she's only tried twice."

Trevor stacked a couple of boxes and hoisted them. "A few times. I told her to butt out."

"You think that works?"

Trevor jerked his chin toward James. "Ask him."

Red flushed James's cheeks. "Let's load up and get these boxes delivered, okay? We've got some merry Christmases to deliver from Cowboy Santa and Springs of Living Water."

Kade's brother followed him up the steps and out the door into the parking lot. "I think you should——"

Kade spoke around his box. "I think it's none of your business. Got that?"

"No need to be a jerk about it."

"I'm not. Coming to dinner at Eaglecrest tonight? Sawyer's home."

"No, but I'll be there for Christmas Eve tomorrow."

"See you then." Kade set the remaining boxes in the truck, clambered into the cab, and glanced over at Cheri. "Sorry to make you wait."

"You did warn me. Did you have to pack up the boxes, too?"

He chuckled as he put the truck into gear. "No, other volunteers did that earlier today. It just turned into a gab fest with the guys."

"Trevor looks grouchy."

"He always is."

"Kade..." Her voice faded.

He glanced over to see her studying his face. "Yes?"

"Does God really simply forgive us when we ask, no matter what?"

Kade's heart surged. "He does. Jesus came to pay our penalty. When we ask forgiveness, it's like He covers us so completely that's all God can see. He looks at us and only sees the purity of Jesus."

"I've known that all my life but, somehow, I've always felt I had to measure up on my own. Kind of like if I did *this* much, He'd cover the rest."

"That's not how it works. Anything we can do doesn't begin to be good enough. The only thing we have to do is accept His gift."

"I want to start over," she whispered. "Accept His gift. Accept yours, if you're still offering."

He laid his hand on the console between them, palm up. She stared at it for a long moment before slowly putting hers inside his. He tightened his fingers around hers.

"I'm definitely still offering, sweetheart. Definitely."

CHAPTER 17

C heri snuggled deeper under her duvet the next morning. Down the hallway, she could hear Grandpa stoking the fire. He'd be starting the coffee next. Grandma still tired quickly — so very quickly — but every day she regained a little bit of strength. Harmony would bounce out of bed in her room next to Cheri's any time, but for these few precious minutes, Cheri would savor the peace.

Seven years ago on Christmas Eve, Kade had proposed. She lingered over the memory. They'd been so very much in love. Sure, they'd been young, only twenty-two, but they'd known each other most of their lives and planned to grow up and grow old together. They had so many dreams.

Today, she'd push aside the memories of what she'd ruined when Dillon had enticed her. God had forgiven her, Kade had forgiven her, and she had finally forgiven herself. Today, she and Harmony would spend most of the day at Eaglecrest. Kade would bring her grandparents up for the evening meal if Grandma felt up to it.

In a few days, she and Kade and the kids would go to dinner at the Scarboroughs. Dillon had rolled his eyes when she'd insisted his parents and Kade be present, but finally agreed. She didn't want to think about Dillon, though.

Cheri stretched and sighed like a contented cat, remembering the kisses in the truck when Kade had finally dropped her off last night, snow drifting down outside the steamed-up windows. She'd watched him deliver box after box to families and seniors in need. Watched worry-worn faces light up with relieved joy at the sight of a small turkey and fixings along with a wrapped gift for each family member. Kade had sheepishly left a box at Paradise Creek, too, but suggested she keep the turkey frozen for another occasion, since they'd be having dinner at Eaglecrest. Then he'd stressed the gifts in the box were from Springs of Living Water, not him.

She glanced at her bedside clock and frowned at the blank face. Oh, no. Was the power out again? How much had it snowed overnight, anyway? She rose, pulled on a pair of fuzzy socks and her cozy robe, then peered out the window to a snowy world. Only the antenna of her car peeked out from the fluffy white cap. Large flakes continued to drift from the sky.

It was gorgeous. And, this time, they were much better prepared for an outage. Thanks to Kade, enough wood was split and stacked to last the winter through.

Enough cans of diesel sat in the generator shed to keep them powered for several weeks.

Cheri hurried into Harmony's room and pulled the blankets off her daughter's bed. "Come on, honey! We've had a ton of fresh snow. Want to come outside and play for a bit before I make breakfast?"

KADE WHISTLED as he forked hay into the horses' feeders. He patted Nip's nose. "Want to pull a sleigh this afternoon, big guy?"

The Percheron whinnied and nuzzled Kade's shoulder.

Kade grinned. "I take that as a yes. Well, eat up. We'll get to it in a bit."

When he returned to the main barn, Sawyer growled at him. "Why are you in such a good mood?"

"Why not?" Kade clouted his brother on the shoulder. "Done hauling feed for the cows?"

"Yeah. I don't get you, bro. How'd you get to be the happy one? Trevor's like a bear woke up in the middle of winter." Sawyer grimaced. "And I know I've got a burr stuck under the saddle. What's with you, anyway?"

"I'm content." Kade dropped to a bale and took off his hat, turning it in his hands. "I believe that if I follow God to the best of my ability and trust Him, He'll take care of me. There's no use fighting life. Trust me, I've tried."

Sawyer leaned against a post in the middle of the

barn. "You've had some rough times. Mostly woman-induced."

Kade nodded. "No regrets, though."

"Yeah? You'd have picked the path where Cheri ran off with Dillon a week before your wedding?"

"That's not exactly what happened, and no, I wouldn't have picked it. She went through a lot of pain there, and so did I. But I also know it happened, and it can't be undone. That situation only has continued power over us if we let it." He shrugged. "I choose not to let it. I choose to look forward and see what God has for me now."

"You're going to ask her to marry you again, aren't you?"

Kade couldn't have stopped the grin even if he wanted to. "Sure am. Soon." He eyed his brother. "Anyone in your life?"

Sawyer shook his head. "Too busy with the rodeo circuit for more than a fling or two."

The implications were best ignored, at least for now. "How long are you going to keep chasing trophies? When is enough success enough?"

"Not sure." Sawyer sighed. "You know what's tough?"

Eyebrows raised, Kade waited.

"Being your kid brother. You're so stinkin' perfect it's sickening. When I'm out on the rodeo circuit, at least you're not there showing me up."

He kept the grin in place. "Never could out-rope you."

"True that." Sawyer eyed him. "It's not that I don't

like you. I do. Everyone does. But why do you have to be such a nice guy?"

Kade chuckled. "Only by the grace of God. You might want to try talking to Him again. Faith keeps a man from needing to prove everything on his own. I just live my life as best I can, trying to honor Him, and let Him take care of the rest."

"Seemed easier when I was a kid."

"Yeah. I hear you. It may be simple, but that doesn't mean it's easy. I pray for you, Sawyer. That you'll find your worth in Him instead of trophies. You know there's room for you on the ranch. Dad never planned for just Trevor and me to run this spread."

"And now you're adding on Paradise Creek."

Kade shrugged. "I guess the spread will be part of the deal, yeah. But you know that's not why I want to marry Cheri. I love her." He chuckled. "And Jer loves Harmony."

"Don't know that I want a woman tying me down, even if she comes with a ranch."

"First things first, bro. Get the foundational stuff figured out with God. Then you might not feel like love ties you down. You might find it sets you free."

Sawyer shook his head. "You're weird. You know that?"

"It works for me." Kade heaved off the bale he'd been sitting on. "Time to head in. Ruthie's probably got breakfast on."

CHERI INHALED THE COLD, damp air as the sleigh, drawn by Nip and Tuck, eased to a stop at the top of the bluff. The view from up here had always drawn her. The creek her ranch was named for tumbled into the river below as it churned from the tree-clad mountains above Eaglecrest to the Montana plains below. The absolute stillness settled over her. She sighed.

Kade shifted on the wooden seat next to her, his thigh pressed against hers. She half expected him to slide an arm around her and pull her close, but then she remembered the children tucked into the backseat. He'd been careful not to do more than hold her hand in front of the little ones.

He cleared his throat. "Harmony, I have a question for you."

"Yes, Mr. Kade?"

Cheri's heart stilled as she stared straight ahead to the gap in the trees where the old wagon trail continued its way to Eaglecrest. She could feel Kade's gaze on the side of her face, but no way was she looking.

"You know your mom and I have known each other a long time, right? Since we were kids not much older than you."

Silence.

Maybe Kade got his answer by way of a nod, because he kept talking. "Once, a long time ago, we were even going to be married, but we didn't. Now, I'm so glad your mom and you are back at the ranch and we've been able to spend time together again."

He wouldn't. Not this way. But it made sense, somehow.

"I like living here."

"I love your mom, Harmony. I want to marry her and be your daddy. I want you to be Jericho's big sister. I want us all to live in one house together and be a family. What do you think of that?"

Against her will, Cheri's hand crept the few inches over and rested on Kade's knee. His fingers covered hers, and he squeezed lightly.

"Can I have a horse?"

A flush crept up Cheri's cheeks. Was her daughter actually bargaining?

"I'm pretty sure we could make a horse part of the deal, if your mom agrees."

"And you'd be my dad? Mom said I already have one I have to meet."

"That's true." Kade's fingers caressed Cheri's. "But I think there's room for me, too. And you'd be my daughter."

"That sounds nice."

Cheri's heart skipped a beat as she closed her eyes. He'd turn to her next. But no.

"Hey, bucko. Would you like Miss Cheri to be your mommy?"

"Her Mama?"

He'd heard what Harmony called her. Cheri's lips quivered as tears puddled in her eyes.

"Yes, Jer. You could call her Mama if you wanted. And Harmony would be your sister."

"Ha'mony sitter?"

"Would you like that?"

"Like."

Cheri turned to Kade, her heart flowing over. "I can't believe..."

His arm came around the back of the bench, his hand rubbing her shoulder as he pulled her closer and pressed a kiss to the hair on her temple. "Cheri Mackenzie, I love you. Will you marry me?" His voice broke. "Will you be a mom to Jericho and let me be a father to Harmony?"

"Kade, I..." She sniffled.

His thumb gently wiped a tear from her cheek.

"Nothing would make me happier. I love you, Kade Delgado. You're everything my heart desires."

His hand lifted her chin, and his deep dark eyes glimmered with emotion. "I love you." And his mouth pressed against hers, gently and sweetly.

"Kiss?" Jericho smacked his lips in the backseat.

Harmony giggled.

Cheri chuckled against Kade's lips as they lifted in a grin.

"More later," he promised in a whisper before releasing her. He flicked the reins. "Walk on."

It was already the best Christmas Eve ever, and it had only just begun.

K ade fidgeted in his black jeans and black shirt. Even his cowboy hat and boots were black... and brand new. Must be the bolo tie with its silver and turquoise slide that made him feel faint, like the air on top of the bluff had been cut off.

Dozens of chairs had been hauled to the hilltop and set out in rows facing the gazebo he'd built during the snowy winter months. His mom had taken charge of decorating the setting in a minimalist way, at his insistence.

Guests from Saddle Springs and Cheri's previous home in Arcadia Valley filled the rows. Beside Kade, Trevor and Sawyer rocked back and forth on their boot heels while James played unending music on the portable organ.

All Kade lacked was a bride, and he tried not to think about how she'd gone missing the last time.

The clop of horses' feet and the jingle of harnesses

reached his craning ears, and he dared to breathe. Two carriages, one half hidden behind the other, creaked into view. Garret drove the more visible one carrying Lauren, Alaina, and Harmony in simple turquoise dresses.

Kade could wait at least another minute to see the inhabitants of the second carriage, Cheri and her grand-parents, driven by Dad and Jericho.

James segued into processional music, and Alaina, Cheri's best friend from Arcadia Valley, strolled down the grassy aisle. On her way to the gazebo, she blew a kiss to her husband, who was holding a baby girl with their twin sons on either side.

By then Lauren had started forward. From the organ, James watched her with hungry eyes. Kade forced himself to pay attention to Lauren rather than James. No amount of cajoling had convinced his friend to test the friendship with the request of more.

Then Harmony and Jericho started forward, Harmony tossing petals in a careful arc until Jericho grabbed her ribbon-bedecked basket and dumped it over. Harmony stood stock still, her lip quivering. Kade sympa-thized. The little guy didn't play by the rules.

Jericho pulled Harmony forward. "Daddy, I come!" Then he let go of Harmony's hand and ran forward, crashing into Kade's knees and nearly taking him out.

A ripple of laughter rolled over the assembly, but Alaina walked back to Harmony and knelt beside her, whispering to her. Then she took the little girl's hand and accompanied her to the gazebo.

Kade held out his hand to Harmony, and she nestled against his other side. "It's okay, sweetie," he whispered.

"I wanted it to be pretty."

"I know. You did a good job for your mama. Don't worry."

She sniffled, but the sound faded as Kade's gaze riveted on the vision that was Cheri in a knee-length white gown, covered in lace. She had a hand tucked through Chester's arm and another through Edith's as they strolled toward him. Her bouquet rested on the top step of the gazebo, waiting for her.

The moment was finally here. Today Kade would marry the love of his life. They'd escape for a whirlwind honeymoon, leaving his brothers and the ranch hands to finish the calving season without him, and when they returned, they'd break ground right here on the bluff for a house fit for their family.

As Cheri and her grandparents paused at the foot of the gazebo, Kade strode down the steps to receive his bride. She was gorgeous. She was glowing. And, miracle of miracles, she loved him.

ACKNOWLEDGMENTS

What is more romantic than sleigh rides and carols during the Christmas season? Not much! I hope you enjoyed experiencing a Saddle Springs Christmas from a snowstorm to the Sunday School Christmas concert to remembering the true joy of Jesus' birth.

Many thanks to Kimberly Rose Johnson for your invitation to a digital Christmas box set. Without that bump, I'm not sure when the town of Saddle Springs, Montana, would have landed on the map. Also big thanks to fellow authors Elizabeth Maddrey and Janet W. Ferguson for exchanging beta reading, and to the other authors who participated in *A Christmas to Remember*.

I appreciate my beta readers: Paula, Amy, Joy, Debbie, and Karen. Thanks for loving this new direction, encouraging me, and catching my errors... although I'm sure I managed to leave a few in, even after my fabulous editor, Nicole, had her input. Thanks for sticking with me through all these years and stories, Nicole.

If you've read previous stories of mine, you'll know that cowboy romance is a slight variation on my usual themes of farm-and-garden such as in my Farm Fresh Romance series and its spinoff series, the Urban Farm Fresh Romances. You may have noticed a nod to my Garden Grown Romances (part of the multi-author Arcadia Valley Romance series), where Cheri Mackenzie played a small role.

Good news! There will be more chronicles in the Montana Ranches Christian Romance series. We'll continue with James and Lauren's story in *The Cowboy's Mixed-Up Matchmaker*. As always, this series links in with my other series, so I hope you'll follow along.

Enjoy this Book?

Please leave a review at any online retailer or reader site. Letting other readers know what you think about *The Cowboy's Christmas Reunion: a Montana Ranches Christian Romance* helps them make a decision and means a lot to me. Thank you!

Keep reading for the first chapter of *The Cowboy's Mixed-Up Matchmaker*, the second book in the Montana Ranches Christian Romance series.

Montana
Ranches
Christian Romance Series

THE
COWBOY'S
Mixed-Up Matchmaker

SADDLE SPRINGS ROMANCE - BOOK 2

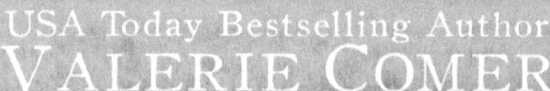

USA Today Bestselling Author
VALERIE COMER

CHAPTER 1

D id you hear Denae Archibald is coming back to town?"

James Carmichael stifled a groan. Why wouldn't Lauren Yanovich let up trying to find him a date? The closer he got to thirty, the more determined she seemed. On the flip side, the closer he got to thirty, the less interested he was in her games.

"Everything looks good." The veterinarian stripped off her gloves and looked up at him as she patted Snowball's flank.

"Uh..." Was Lauren talking about the horse... or Denae? It was never safe to assume. James tore his gaze from Lauren and stroked the filly's forelock. "Great. Glad to hear it."

"Denae is a sought-after editor now. Who knew, right? But she was always so good at everything she tried." Lauren lathered up in the stable's deep sink.

"I haven't spent two minutes in the past decade wondering what happened to Denae."

Lauren chuckled but didn't look up. "That's because you haven't seen her lately. She's drop dead gorgeous. She was even first runner-up at the Miss Snowflake contest over in Helena last Christmas."

"I'm thrilled for her." Hopefully, the bland way he said the words would hush Lauren up.

"You should be. She's going to be renting the other half of my duplex from me starting April first—"

"Ah ha, an April Fool's joke. Nice one, Lauren."

She dried on a scrap of old towel, glancing at James as she shook her head. "You're not getting any younger."

He shrugged. Didn't he know it. Most guys probably dreaded the big three-oh but, for him, it presented an opportunity. A crossroads. His gut roiled at the thought. He should probably purchase shares in an antacid company, with the amount he was going through lately. Or at least buy them by the case. If only he could do something about the situation now, but it was bad timing. It was always a bad time with Lauren focused on match-making. He followed her outside, like a pup after a scent.

Lauren rested both arms on the corral rails and took a deep breath as she gazed toward the Bitterroots. "I always love coming out to the Flying Horseshoe. It's so peaceful."

"You say that like Saddle Springs is a big city," he teased. "When we're full up here in the summer, the ranch's population nearly rivals the town's." She was right, though. His parents' ranch lay tucked in the foothills of western Montana, rolling and picturesque with its small lake. Good thing they'd been able to repurpose the vast acres from working ranch to guest ranch after Dad's accident when James was in college. He'd quit, coming home to pitch in. Never regretted it for a minute. This was his home. His destiny.

"You know what I mean."

He braced beside her, allowing the sleeve of his denim shirt to brush against her navy coveralls. He couldn't feel her arm through all that fabric. Even less when she shifted slightly away.

"I get it." All of it. He stared up to where a few dark clouds shrouded the peaks. Snow again? It was never too late, not in the mountains. They'd even had a dusting in July that one year. Thankfully his best bud's outdoor wedding had gone off without a hitch last weekend.

That only reminded James of Lauren wearing a shapely calf-length turquoise dress, carrying a bouquet of sunny daffodils and white tulips down the grassy aisle. He couldn't remember the last time he'd seen her in a dress. Prom, maybe? At any rate, he hadn't been able to tear his eyes away.

Ask her out already, dude. His friend's voice rang in his memory.

James glanced at Lauren. Her short dark hair curled around her head, a sensible cut for a veterinarian. The coveralls were sensible, too. The jeans and baggy sweatshirts she usually wore probably fit the same label. When had the life of their high school class become *sensible*?

"There's a new waitress at the Branding Iron. Pretty with long blond hair."

Obviously there was no way Lauren would go out with James. She did everything to get rid of even his friendship. He scowled at her. "Yeah? Why are you telling me this?"

"Because you're—"

"Stop reminding me of my age."

She pulled back at the harshness in his voice. "Sor*ree*. Just trying to help."

"Don't. Just don't."

"I thought you'd probably want to get married and have a batch of little cowpokes running around to keep your nephew company."

"Maybe someday."

She bit her lip. Her pretty, full lip. The one he craved to taste.

"Besides, what about you?" James trod on dangerous ground, now. He didn't actually want to push her away, but her matchmaking needed to stop. Like, yesterday.

"Me?" Lauren tossed her head. "Too busy. With the expansion of the Saddle View subdivision, we've got dozens more horses in the area, many with inexperienced owners. Lots of calls out that way, to say nothing of the usual."

He hated to see her overworked and tired. "Is Doc Torrington putting too much pressure on you? Maybe you guys should hire another vet."

"No, we're good. I've got nothing else to do with my time."

"If you had more time, you could date."

Lauren laughed. "Back around, are we?"

"Well, yeah. As you keep telling me, thirty's coming. As I recall, we share a birthday." Like he'd ever forgotten.

"Maybe we should have a party!" Her hazel eyes sparkled.

"A... what?"

"Surely you've heard of parties. Where a bunch of friends get together and have a good time, often to celebrate a special occasion?"

What he really had in mind was a private dinner for two where he offered his heart in completion of the pledge he'd made on their sixteenth birthday, just after Dillon Scarborough had broken up with her. She'd been crushed.

Good friends don't let friends turn thirty... single.

They'd even high-fived on it.

Even then, he'd adored the ground she walked on. He'd never dreamed that thirteen-and-a-half years later, he might have the chance to redeem his pledge.

She'd probably turn him down. Laugh in his face. She didn't want to marry anyone. She constantly pushed him off on someone else. But, didn't a guy have to try?

Everything on the line.

He'd been working toward the final test of that motto forever.

If he only knew.

Right. Lauren muffled a snort. If he did, he'd laugh his head off, and she couldn't bear that. Nope, her best bet was to carry on as she'd begun, trying to find James's perfect match. When he was safely married off, she could relax — yeah, sure — and focus on her work. She'd even teach his kids in Sunday School, no problem.

Okay, it would be a problem, but she'd do it anyway, because Saddle Springs was home, and she wasn't going anywhere. Neither, apparently, was he. Somebody needed to get married and put her out of her misery. Had to be him.

James's sister came around the corner of the stable, leading a black gelding. "Hey, Lauren."

Whew. Good diversion. "Hiya, Tori. Good-looking boy. He new here?"

Tori nodded. "His name is Coaldust. We just picked him up from a ranch over near Polson."

Lauren took in the gelding's conformation and bright eyes. "How old is he?"

"Five. Saddle broke with an easy gait. I think he'll be a favorite with guests this summer."

Coaldust tossed his head with a little whinny.

Lauren dug in her pocket for the apple chunk left over from Snowball and held it out to Coaldust. He eyed her as though to determine whether she was friend or foe before nipping it off her palm. She rubbed his velvety nose and crooned soft nothings to him as his ears twitched.

As fidgety as James shifting at her side. He was sure acting odd today... or was he? He'd slid into somewhat moody and unpredictable behavior over the past few months, or maybe even longer. They used to talk for hours, about anything and everything. Well, nearly. A girl needed her secrets. But things had changed, and she couldn't figure out why.

At first, Lauren had thought he'd fallen in love and was thus avoiding her. She'd braced herself for the introduction to his girlfriend and seeing his eyes light up for the other woman, but time went on, and it hadn't happened. It needed to happen, as much as she dreaded it. Once he'd moved on, she could, too. Right?

"...wouldn't that be fun?"

Lauren blinked, refocusing on Tori. "Um, sorry. Wool-gathering. What did you say?"

"Never mind," James said quickly. "Bad idea."

"I think it's a great idea." Tori pouted at her brother and turned back to Lauren. "I was thinking a few of us should get together for a weekend getaway before the summer rush begins. We could ride way back above the Flying Horseshoe and into the National Forest. Camp for a couple of days by the geothermal pool." She elbowed Lauren. "I'll share my tent with you."

James's face shuttered. "Too much going on."

What on earth was he thinking? Lauren angled a look at him. "It was a ton of fun when we used to do it." So many good memories from before he became owly.

He shrugged.

Men. Lauren turned to Tori. "Let me know what weekend you're looking at, and I'll see if I can book it off. Who all are you thinking of inviting?"

Tori glanced between them. "Well, us three, of course. We could ask Cheri and Kade. I think Sawyer

Delgado is away on the rodeo circuit, but Trevor might be interested."

Trevor would most likely cast a wet blanket on the trip, but that was no more than James was already doing. Who could be counted on for amusement? "Oh, I bet Denae Archibald would love to come. She's moving back April first."

James groaned.

"Nice. And maybe Carmen Haviland?" Tori tapped her jaw. "Possibly Garret Morrison."

"Sounds like a fun group. Are you thinking of including the little ones? Cheri and Kade can probably get his mom to watch their kids, but I'm not sure whether Carmen can get away."

"I can't believe you're talking as though this is a real thing."

Tori jammed her elbow into her brother's side. "Why not? I only got to go along that one time and then you guys quit doing it. Before that, I was just the little tagalong no one wanted."

"We were all kids then."

Lauren chuckled. "I'm pretty sure I'm not too old or out-of-shape to sit in the saddle for a few hours on a mountain trail. If *you* are..."

He scowled at her. "You don't know what you're talking about, woman."

"Well, either you can handle trailriding, or you can't."

"It's not about being horseback."

She raised her eyebrows, not daring to read anything

into his piercing glare. "Then what? I happen to know you can cook."

"I have to say he's out of practice." Tori giggled.

He whooshed out a long breath and looked between them. "I just want to go on record as saying it's a bad idea. Okay?" Then he strode away.

She dared watch his fine form until he disappeared into the end guest cabin he'd claimed for his own a couple of years ago, the scuffed boots, snug jeans, denim shirt stretched over broad shoulders, and his dark cowboy hat etched in her memory along with all the other sightings.

"Man, he's like a bear stumbling out of a leaky cave in the middle of winter," Tori observed. "He's been such a grouch for the past few months. Even worse since Kade and Cheri's wedding. Wasn't that dreamy?" She sighed. "Talk about a happy ending."

"James is probably pining for a good love story of his own," Lauren said lightly. "I was thinking he and Denae might hit it off, so your idea of a camping trip is great timing."

Tori tilted her head and regarded Lauren. "Interesting thought. I've sometimes wondered why he hasn't latched onto a gorgeous woman of his own. I mean, the grumpiness is off-putting, I'm sure, but he's decently good-looking. If a kid sister is allowed to say so."

"I've seen uglier. At least he doesn't have a wart on his nose." Lauren forced out a chuckle. "He probably just hasn't met the right girl yet. When he does, he'll move so quickly your head will spin."

Tori giggled. "You're probably right. So, what's your

work schedule like? How many weekends do you get off? Then I'll start calling around to see who's in, and we'll go from there."

Lauren pulled out her phone and opened the calendar app, sharing the info with Tori.

"Great. I'll be in touch." Tori thumbed over her shoulder toward James's cabin. "And if Mr. Grumpy doesn't want to come along, we can have a great time without him."

"Yeah! We sure can." Lauren slapped Tori's raised palm. "I'd better get back to the clinic and see what other calls we've got. Keep me in the loop."

"Will do."

Lauren climbed into her Jeep Wrangler and shot one more glance at James's cabin. A good time camping without him? Definitely not. There'd be a huge gap if he didn't come. It wasn't just his voice lifted around the campfire during the sing-along she'd miss. She'd miss his easy way in the forest, building a fire, helping everyone out with all the little things in camp, making everything run smoothly. She'd miss filling her eyes and mind with his handsome — if somewhat moody — face.

No. What she'd really miss was the chance to hook him up with Denae.

ABOUT THE AUTHOR

Valerie Comer lives where food meets faith in her real life, her fiction, and on her blog and website. She and her husband of over 35 years farm, garden, and keep bees on a small farm in Western Canada, where they grow and preserve much of their own food.

Valerie has always been interested in real food from scratch, but her conviction has increased dramatically since God blessed her with four delightful granddaughters. In this world of rampant disease and pollution, she is compelled to do what she can to make these little girls' lives the best she can. She helps supply healthy food — local food, organic food, seasonal food — to grow strong bodies and minds.

Valerie is a *USA Today* bestselling author and a two-time Word Award winner. She is known for writing engaging characters, strong communities, and deep faith laced with humor into her green clean romances.

To find out more, visit her website www.valeriecomer.com where you can read her blog, and explore her many links. You can also find Valerie blogging with other authors of Christian contemporary romance at Inspy Romance.

Why not join her email list where you will find news, giveaways, deals, book recommendations, and more? Your thank-you gift is *Promise of Peppermint*, the prequel novella to the Urban Farm Fresh Romance series.

http://valeriecomer.com/subscribe